A Pocketful
of Rye

A Pocketful
of Rye

by A. J. Cronin

Little, Brown and Company · Boston · Toronto

A Pocketful
of Rye

one

THE EXPRESS LETTER came late in the afternoon.

I was standing comfortably with Matron Müller on the terrace of the clinic, putting on my usual act of kindly interest as the children packed into the big green departure coach that would take them through the mountains by the Echberg Pass to Basle for the chartered night flight back to Leeds. It hadn't rained much during their six weeks and the little runts looked well and full of themselves, packing the open side windows to shout *auf Wiedersehen* and other picked-up bits of Schweizerdeutsch. They were waving the paper Swiss flags that Matron always handed out with sample bars of patriotic milk chocolate. As the coach rolled down the drive they began to sing "Lili Marlene." They had picked that up too, endlessly playing the old scratched record in the playroom.

"Well, that's the last batch of summer, Matron," I remarked on a poetic note, as the coach disappeared behind a frieze of firs. "They weren't bad brats."

7

"*Ach, Herr Doktor.*" She raised a reproving finger, but fondly. "Vy must you use that vort. Brats. These last were goot child-ern and for me a goot child is the handvork of Gott."

"But Matron," I improvised quickly, "brat is just an affectionate English idiom. In Britain people of the highest rank will publicly refer to their offspring as brats."

"Ach, zo? You are serious?"

"I assure you."

"Zo! A fun affection. An English odium of vellborn people."

"Exactly."

Her small eyes approved me indulgently. Hulda Müller was a short, thick woman of about sixty, her architecture late Victorian, with a magnificent portico. Thorny gray hair protruded from her white stringed cap, her faint moustache was discreetly powdered. Draped to the heels in the shapeless white gown to which the cantonal nurses were condemned, she was the genuine Schweizer article. Correct, hygienic, humorless, unutterably dull, and while not, in the cheap sense of the word, a snob, imbued with an inherent Germanic reverence for rank. But capable and industrious, a worker fifteen hours a day, coping with shortage of staff in the ward and the kitchen, feeding me as I had never, in my spotty down-at-heel career, been fed before.

"It is highly agreeable to me that you make explanations of such odiums, Herr Doktor Carroll. You, a person knowing and yourself coming from the *Hochgeboren*."

"A pleasure, Matron. You'll have all the odium I'm capable of."

Oh, careful, you clown, don't push it too far. I flashed a smile at her, loaded with charm. In any institution it is the first rule of life to be in with the matron. And since my heaven-sent arrival seven months ago I had worked diligently on Hulda, soaping her with some inspired fictions, creating a few noble ancestors to strengthen my image. So now this fire-breathing old dragon, this veteran of the bedpans, this Hippocratic priestess in a white soutane was entirely mine or, rather, I was hers—her bright-eyed *Junge*.

"Now ve have the six veeks' pause," she reflected. "You vill re-commence your postgraduates at the Zürich Kantonspital?"

"I'll go down at least once or twice a week," I agreed thoughtfully. "Beginning on Tuesday."

"Ach, it is goot to have the charge of a young, eager, scientific doktor. Our late Herr Doktor vas . . ." she shook her head, *"ein Schrinker."*

"Das war nicht gut für Sie," I responded, demonstrating my advance in colloquial German.

"Nein, aber das ist ein Problem für seine neue Frau." The law that married doctors were unacceptable at the clinic thus defined, she examined the watch dangling from her bosom. "But now I must go to see for your tea." Moving off she glanced at me archly. "You like perhaps these ramekins I make special for you."

9

"Matron, they're a dream and you . . . you're a regular 'dreamboat.'"

She giggled, not amused, just pleased.

"Dreambote? That's goot?"

"The best."

When she had gone I suddenly felt annoyed with myself. In her own way she was kind and decent. And shouldn't I be thanking my lucky star to be here? On velvet at last after eight years of mucking around in the worst kinds of General Practice.

When I graduated at Winton University I had taken a voyage to Australia as ship's doctor in a cargo boat, then come back all set for the quick trip to Harley Street. It did not take long to demonstrate the financial and professional worth of a low-grade Scots degree. Who wants you with that, with the dung of the kailyard on your boots, and the porridge still stuck to your chaps? At first a few locums, one in the Highlands with a hard-drinking member of the MacDuff clan, then a short assistantship, followed by another locum in the slums of Winton where, half starved, I worked overtime for an obese old sloth who staggered back from his holiday at Glendrum Hydro loaded with the menu cards for every meal, immediately sat down, still drooling all over his paunch, and one by one read them out to me.

Then came a long assistantship in Nottingham with the vague view to a partnership that was never meant to materialize. But why elaborate the sorry record: the long hours in sweaty surgeries, the night calls, the health insurance cards to be faked after-hours, the scanty, irregular, oven-desiccated meals, the unequal division of labor smugly passed off with: "Oh, by the way, Carroll, my wife and I are going out to dinner and the theater. You won't mind polishing off these three late calls that have just come in."

And not every wife was taken out to dinner. "I often think I am wasting the best years of my life in Sudsbury, Dr. Carroll. Sydney is so wrapped up in his practice; you must see that—for a young man you are so understanding." Slipping me an extra slice of scraggy mutton under the mashed potatoes, with a lingering look, while Sydney had his mug in the *B.M.J.* Poor plump, but fading yearner. I helped you with kind words alone. How could one find romance in those droopy drawers strung out every other Monday in the Sudsbury backyard?

My last stretch hit mud bottom when, as obstetric physician—so called—in a Medical Aid practice in the South Wales Rhondda Valley, knocked up by the midwife most nights of the week, staggering out into the shadow world of endless miners' rows half dressed and still half asleep to grope up the ladder to the attic, clash on the forceps and pull, I seemed to be a robot performer, perhaps the cymbalist, in a bizarre symphony of sweat, tears, filth and blood.

It was in the murky dawn after such a night, as I stood on the concrete floor of the central surgery, still in my professional rig of pajamas, old overcoat and pit clogs, wrapping a bottle of ergot—that panacea for the reluctant placenta—in a disemboweled page from the

Lancet, that my bloodshot eye was caught by a small strip advertisement on the half-torn page.

> WANTED: *For the Maybelle Children's Clinic and Holiday Home, Schlewald, Switzerland, as Medical Superintendent, British doctor, single and preferably under 30. Knowledge of German and pulmonary lesions a recommendation. Full board and comfortable quarters provided. Salary £500 per annum, payable in Sterling or Swiss francs. Further particulars and application forms from J. Scrygemour & Co. Solicitors, Halifax, Yorks.*

I stood there, hypnotized, with a kind of prevision that this was precisely what I needed, wanted, and must have. And yet, as I stared through the dirty dispensary window, hung over by the gallows outline of mine headstocks against the coal tips, I did not fail to comprehend that normally I hadn't an earthly. Nevertheless, a strange feeling had begun to form at the back of my mind that this was no fortuitous intervention in my life, that here was an opportunity specially designed for Laurence Carroll and one which I must take. Compulsively, I sat down and wrote to J. Scrygemour & Co.

The reply came within three days.

The clinic was a foundation from the estate of Mrs. Bella Keighley, widow of a wealthy North of England cotton spinner, who had settled in Schlewald with her daughter Maybelle in the year 1896. The daughter was delicate, a consumptive case, consigned for the short

12

span of her life to an Alpine existence. When she died some years later the mother, for sentimental reasons, or from a genuine attachment to Switzerland, had continued her Schlewald domicile, and on her death, under the terms of the will, the large chalet had been extended, a ward of twelve beds and a number of small out-chalets constructed and the establishment set up for the benefit of underprivileged British children, "particularly those suffering from weakness or disorders of the lungs." The staff consisted of the resident doctor, matron, and probationer nurse.

Six times a year batches of children were received for convalescence or holidays. Those requiring further treatment were retained in the ward.

Two weeks later I went to Halifax for the interview, which took place at the Scrygemour office in Market Street. Naturally I was nervous, yet in view of the preparations I had made, and for which I trust no one will misjudge me, not altogether lacking in hope. Four other candidates were in the waiting room, not a bad-looking lot, in fact two had London degrees considerably better than mine, but when I sounded them it appeared that, of the four, none could speak German. So far so good. Before I went in, last, I took a final glance at the old tourists' phonetic phrase book I had found secondhand in Cardiff and been mugging up for the past ten days, then tapped respectfully on the frosted panel of the door.

The committee had three members: Scrygemour, who was small, benevolent and shiningly bald, and two solid Yorkshire businessmen of the stand-no-

nonsense school. When they had looked me over, the interrogation began. I was in my best form—quiet, alert, convincing, modestly forthcoming yet personally reserved—not pressing the advantages I had thought up, letting them winkle all the good points out of me as though it embarrassed me mildly to acknowledge them. Yes, I admitted I liked children, had always got on well with them, not only as one of a large family but in my extensive practice. At a mention of the excellence of my testimonials I betrayed no surprise—naturally enough, since I had composed two of the better ones myself. Yes, I agreed calmly, a South Wales colliery town was not perhaps socially the most desirable field of action for an ambitious young man. Yet, oddly enough, it *was:* I had purposely chosen that location to study the pneumokoniosis, adding a moment later when this floored them: "Which, as you obviously know, gentlemen, comprises the pulmonary diseases—anthracosis, silicosis, and tuberculosis—specially affecting workers in the mining industry."

An impressive silence followed this well-thought-out gambit. After glancing at the other two, Scrygemour remarked: "That is a point of considerable interest to us, Dr. Carroll." Then, diffidently as though scarcely hoping, he cleared his throat:

"I don't suppose you would happen to know German, Doctor?"

I smiled, staking my entire position on the clincher. Either I was in, or out flat on my ear.

"Aber, mein Herr, Ich können der Deutsch gude."

It knocked them cold—they hadn't one word of

14

German among them. And before they could recover I let them have a few more fluent, though not particularly appropriate cuttings from my little green book.

"Entschuldigen Sie, mein Herr, können Sie mir zeigen wo das nächste Abort ist?" (Excuse me, sir, can you direct me to the nearest lavatory?)

"Zimmermädchen, ich glaube unter meinem Bett ist eine Maus." (Chambermaid, I think there is a mouse under my bed.)

"Very satisfactory, Doctor. Very." This actually from one of the hard types. "May we ask how you acquired such proficiency in the language?"

"Mainly from my study of pulmonary diseases in the original German textbooks," I murmured, knowing that I was home, even before they had me in again, after a short wait outside, to congratulate me and shake me warmly by the hand.

Of course, it was a thoroughly discreditable performance. It was cheap, contemptible, despicable, downright dishonest. But when you have been on the verge of the breadline and been kicked around for seven years your sense of ethics becomes somewhat blunted. And although next morning I was prepared to cry *"mea culpa, mea maxima culpa,"* I was happy, that same afternoon, to be packing my bag for Schlewald. After all, in my usual fashion, I could try to exonerate myself. The Jesuits, who were partly responsible for my schooling, had, in the brief term of our relationship which occurred when I was extremely young, imbued me with their most practical principle, that the end justifies the means. And in utilizing my only means of

15

persuasion upon these worthy Yorkshiremen I was no more than accomplishing a necessary act to achieve a necessary end.

So at least, for the moment, let us admit that I was safely here in Schlewald, happily anchored in the Maybelle Clinic, breathing the delicious mountain air and gazing about me with a mildly proprietory air. It was one of those perfect Alpine afternoons that lit the landscape with a pale translucent blue. In the pasture before the clinic, which stood high on the southern slope, autumn crocuses, still unfolded, stained the vivid green where rivulets of cold clear water tumbled over each other downhill to the river. In the pinewoods across the valley the toy train that ran to Davos had begun its slow vertiginous climb, turning on its own tail, stopping now on a loop of the higher grade as though to recover steam, but actually to allow the Davos down train to pass. Above, on the scar of the Gotschna Grat, a faint dusting of early snow was already anticipating the sunset, turning from gold to a rich rose madder. Distantly, and far below, dwarfed by the mountain, the rooms of Schlewald Dorf looked cozy, *gemütlich* was the word. Lush descriptions apart, it was a sweet spot, and when you thought of those miners' rows, the slag heaps without a blade of grass, the surgery bell going day and night and Tonypandy Blodwen croaking in your half-awakened ear: "Eh, doctor bach, I'm mortal sorry to 'ave you out again but it's a britch and I canna' get the 'ead away"—well, it was peaceful as a bottle of tranquilizers. I liked it here, in fact I was completely sold on it.

A young moon, pale as a sliver of Emmenthaler in the persistent light, was beginning to slide over the ridge and suddenly from across and far away came the sound of an Alpine horn. A herdsman sitting by his lonely hut on the upper pastures with that ridiculous six-foot wooden tube which, like the Scottish bagpipes, is hideous near the eardrums but which, floating down from the hills, has a magic all its own. Again it came, vibrating in the still air. It hits you, that prolonged deep sadness, losing itself in the distance, silenced by the peaks. It cuts the cord, and suddenly you too are lost. You sink into yourself, and given a chance, some secret misery sneaks up from your subconscious.

With me it is always the same—a torment and a mystery—I am in that dark empty street of an unknown city and in the dead silence of the night I hear footfalls behind me, slow, persistent, menacing. I cannot turn round and must sweat out the agony of that unknown pursuit until suddenly a dog barks and all is still again.

Oh, come off it, Carroll, and stay happy. No one is interested in your private little phobia, at least not yet. It was time for me to get back to my tea and ramekins.

Then, as I turned, I saw someone come through the lodge gates—Hans, the postmaster's son, hurrying up the drive, now waving to me with something in his hand. A letter.

"Express, Rekommende, Herr Doktor." It was probably my monthly check and for this the Swiss post never keeps you waiting.

He was pretending to be out of breath, but as I was in a soft mood when I signed the receipt, I told him to hold on, went into my sitting room which opened off the terrace. This was a snug little room with a warm red carpet, solid, well polished, comfortable furniture upholstered in brown velveteen, while on the table Matron very thoughtfully kept me supplied with a bowl of the Valais fruits, apricots, pears, apples and cherries, which were so plentiful at this season.

"Catch, Hans." I threw him a big Golden Delicious apple from the open window.

He wouldn't eat it now, I felt sure, but as a true little Swiss, to whom possession is ten points of the law, would take it home, polish it, and keep it—at least until Sunday. I watched him go off with a *vielen Dank, Herr Doktor.*

Then I examined the letter, and was suddenly set back on my heels. It wasn't possible! The envelope was postmarked Levenford, that most distasteful, almost fatal word from which in all its connotations I hoped I had finally cut myself adrift. Reluctantly, I opened the envelope. Yes, from my old playmate Francis Ennis.

My dear Laurence.

I must ask pardon for failing to write congratulating you on your appointment last summer. There was a very pleasing little paragraph in the Winton Herald. May I now, belatedly, wish you every success in your new and most worthy endeavor.

And now I hesitate to proceed. For I am constrained to ask a special favor of you.

18

You remember Cathy Considine, I'm sure, that very sweet companion of our boyhood days who married Daniel Davigan, and was so recently and tragically widowed. Yes, Laurence, theirs was a model marriage, a shining example of marital unity. It was a fearful blow when Dan was taken. You must have seen the account and obituary notice two months ago in the public press; locally, at least, it created quite a stir. And lately, alas, another affliction for the sorrowing widow. The only child, Daniel, just seven years of age, and without question a most remarkable and exceptionally clever little boy, has turned quite poorly. Very pale, glands in the neck and, not to put too fine a point on it, a suspicion of TB. Canon Dingwall, though in retirement and still in his wheelchair following another slight stroke, has shown a great interest in the boy, has brought him along in every way—actually Daniel is two classes ahead of his age—and he has taken the matter up strongly with Dr. Moore who at once suggested a spell, brief we hope, in a sanatorium. All very well to suggest, but here, with the waiting under the new Health Scheme, it would be a good six months before a place could be found for Daniel. And then only in the Grampians, which I dare say bear no comparison with your sunny Swiss Alps.

So it has been decided that Cathy must take the boy to Switzerland and devote herself to his cure. The two dear pilgrims propose leaving here

19

on Tuesday of next week, October 7, arriving Zurich Airport at 5:30 p.m., and as they have no contacts in that city and must feel quite lost, I am relying on you at least to meet them. If you can do nothing further, please see them on their way to Davos, where they have an address from Dr. Moore. But Laurence, if it is at all humanly possible, won't you take charge of them yourself, find a place for Daniel in your clinic, get him well again? Please! For the boy's sake. God will bless you for it, Laurence, and we, all your good friends in Winton, will never cease to thank you.

I read it again, slowly, shuddering slightly over "the dear pilgrims," then instinctively I crushed the letter, tight and hard. What a rocket! What a blasted imposition. Coming after me "for old times' sake," thanking me in advance, handing me the good old heaven will bless you. And spoiling my Tuesday in Zurich, the one day of the week when Svenska Örnflyg were normally free of regular flights.

Yet, how could I give Ennis the brush-off? My name would stink at home. I would have to do something about it, and after all, it was only on a short-term basis. I supposed I must handle it but, as always, I would do so with calm detachment and mature consideration.

two

THE PROBATIONER brought the tea tray into my sitting room, that snug little carpeted den with the easy chair before the blue and white tiled wood stove. She was a fresh country girl from the Valais, smelling pleasantly of the dairy and with well-formed milk bars, who, as she went out, before closing the door always gave me a look over her shoulder not altogether bovine. But today I failed to respond, nor did the fragrant cheesy odor of the fresh-baked ramekins break through my moodiness. Yes, the letter was a nuisance, a confounded nuisance, it had upset me, taking me back to a period in my early life that I was never unduly eager to recall.

Personally, I cannot endure throwbacks, they interrupt the action which is dying to burst forth, but to put the picture in perspective it must be related that at the age of fifteen I had gone to live with my grandparents in Levenford. One month before, with that touch of the absurd apparent to those familiar with the beginnings of my erratic career, I had precociously won the Ellison Bursary to Winton University, an achievement somewhat dulled when it became apparent that to enter the university I must attend Levenford Academy for one year to take the Higher Leaving Certificate examination of the Scottish School Board.

My welcome by the Bruces at their semidetached villa in Woodside Avenue was not effusive. In running off with my Catholic father, their favorite daughter had deeply distressed them. And now, sixteen years later, fulfilling their worst forebodings, they were landed with the sole surviving evidence of that ill-fated union.

My grandfather, Robert Bruce, was an upstanding, dignified burgher of the town, retired on a pension from his position as head of the timber department in the local shipyard of Dennison Brothers, whose staid existence was transfigured by the belief, generally regarded as fictitious, that he was the lineal descendant of the Scottish hero who, after cracking de Bohun's skull with his battle-ax in single combat, led the Scots to victory over the English at Bannockburn in 1314—a date I was never permitted to forget.

Do not imagine that my grandfather was either a fool or a laughingstock. He had documents, genealogical trees, extracts from meetings of the local Historical Society, and had traced his family in Levenford as far back as the fifteenth century, a record in which the name Robert was generic. Moreover, Cardross Castle where King Robert I died in 1329 stood by the river Leven on the outskirts of the town and it was from here that Sir James Douglas had set out to take the heart of Bruce to the Holy Land, only to fall, fighting the Moors in Spain. Without digressing further, it is enough to say that my grandfather's obsession, or if you prefer it, delusion, was honest and so deeply felt that he made every year a pilgrimage to Melrose Abbey where the casket containing the heart of King Robert was now enshrined.

Some of this genealogy rubbed onto me and, suitably embroidered, was often socially opportune, but this apart, Bruce treated me always with decent toleration and a fine sense of justice, while my grandmother, a small, bowed wisp of a woman, devoted yet quietly resigned, her head carried patiently to one side—she was slightly deaf—addicted to the Bible, strong tea and the works of Annie S. Swan, and to the habit— to me endearing—of talking soundlessly to herself, her lips moving to the accompaniment of little nods, grimaces and other subtle sympathetic changes of expression, decidedly was, despite the worn-out look of Scottish wives who have served strong men hand and foot, a sweet person.

Levenford Academy, which under the terms of the Bursary I was compelled to attend, was a solid, old-established institution situated in the heart of the borough, with the excellence and all the prejudice of the true-blue Scots grammar school. My advent here was even less welcome, and it was with some relief that I discovered a co-religionist already in my form—Francis Ennis, son of Dr. Ennis. As the only two Papists in the academy we inevitably drew together, not at first from any natural affinity, but simply because we were in the same uncomfortable boat, objects of suspicion and derision to our fellow scholars.

Frank was the only son of a painfully pious mother, a devotee who haunted the church, not merely to wear out her knees before the Stations of the Cross, but as a kind of female sacristan who dressed, adorned, and tended the altar with a holy solicitude that defied the repressive hints, discouraging looks, and even downright prohibitions from the rector of St. Patrick's, the fabulous Canon Dingwall. Unhappily for Frank, his father was a cock of less downy feather. Dr. Ennis, perhaps the best and the hardest worked doctor in town, was a big untidy man with a rough, ribald tongue, a strong addiction to neat whiskey and a fondness for squeezing the dairymaids at the outlying farms he visited. Careless of public opinion, he did as he pleased, and while nominally Catholic, his views on religion were unorthodox, often spectacularly unpredictable. For that matter, using the pretext of his busy practice, he was rarely seen inside the doors of St. Patrick's. It was he who had sent his son to the academy, preparatory to entering him at Edinburgh University where he would take a medical degree and join his father in practice.

Frank was a most prepossessing boy, open and friendly in manner, and quite exceptionally good-looking. Tall, slightly built, with a delicate girlish complexion and thick chestnut hair, he had the bluest long-lashed eyes I had ever seen. In school he was not noticeably clever, rather the reverse, and in his physical contacts with the rougher boys he was inclined to timidity. Although he never complained of this bullying, he had obviously suffered until I was able to take his part. But his one outstanding quality which set him apart was simply this: in the strict sense of the word he was *good*.

One morning during our first week together he was late coming to school and was given a punishment.

"What happened, Frank?" I asked him. "Did you sleep in?"

"Oh, no." He smiled. "Canon Dingwall was held up by a sick call. You see, I serve his seven o'clock Mass every morning."

"What! You do . . . get up so early!"

"It's quite easy once you have the habit."

"I suppose Dingwall's forced you into it. He puts the wind up me."

"You're quite wrong, Laurence. He just seems terribly stern and severe. Once you know him he's the sweetest person."

I glanced at him doubtfully. The Canon, a black, forbidding, hatchet-featured Highlander, six feet two tall and thin as a ramrod, an emaciated Scots Savanarola, towering in the pulpit, scourging his groundling Irish immigrant congregation with an intellectual sardonic wit that bit deeper than mere crude blastings of hellfire, flagellations interposed with sudden ritual snuff-takings during which a pin might be heard to drop in a church packed to suffocation, scarcely struck me as a fount of sweetness and light. He invariably stood at the church door before the eleven o'clock

Mass, had already spotted me, and was undoubtedly aware of my dubious antecedents.

"Every time I pass him he gives me the excommunication stare."

"He just has to put on that kind of act, Laurence. To get results. And he has. All the top Prots, the Dennison brothers especially, think the world of him, the way he's stamped out drunkenness in the town. It was mostly in our lot. But beyond that he's terribly interesting, well read and cultured, a real scholar. He spent five years teaching philosophy at the Scots College in Rome. You'd love him." As I shook my head he smiled and took my arm. "I'll give you a knock down to him after Mass next Sunday."

"Some hope," I said, scornfully. "I'll skip him by going in the side door."

Nevertheless, rather averse myself to morning rising, I respected Frank for this unexpectedly revealed asceticism as I did progressively for other comparable aspects of his character. He never, for example, took the slightest notice of the usual school smut, the lavatory scrawlings, the dirty jokes. And if anyone told a doubtful story in his presence his starry eyes remained fixed on the horizon, the actual meaning of the thing seemed to pass over his head.

All this struck me as commendable, more perhaps as the indication of an original, refined and superior turn of mind than from considerations of morality—since I was probably as venal as the boys he despised. One day, however, a peculiar incident occurred.

I still had a bicycle, from my better days, an old

Rudge Whitworth, and as Francis, whose mother denied him nothing, had a brand new Humber, we began on Saturdays to take rides together into the surrounding country, then quite unspoiled, still wild with the freedom of Scottish hills and heaths. Summer was coming in and as the days got warmer we went further afield, to Malloch and along the winding shore of Loch Lomond to Luss where we bathed. It seemed slightly odd that when we undressed on the warm pebbled beach Frank always moved off a few paces to the shelter of a rock, emerging well covered by a full bathing suit. I did not remark on it, imagining that perhaps he had a mole or some kind of birthmark and was sensitive about it. One day I forgot to bring my pants and, thinking nothing of it, tore off my clothes and dashed into the Loch in a state of nature.

"Come on in," I shouted. "It's wonderful."

There was a pause, then he called back:

"I'm not bathing today."

"Don't you feel well?"

He did not answer.

I took a long swim out to the island. The water was warmer than usual and the sense of being completely naked and unhampered made it even more delicious. When I came back and had dressed Frank came out from behind the rock. He was deeply flushed, his lips set in a firm line.

"You know, of course," he said accusingly, his voice stony, "that it's a sin, almost a mortal one, to expose yourself."

I stared at him in amazement.

27

"And that you make me sin too if I look at you."

I burst out laughing.

"Oh, come off it, Frank. Don't be such a sissy. None of the other boys wear pants, let alone complete bathing suits, and it's far nicer without. You must try it."

"I won't," he shouted, beginning to tremble. "Never."

"Oh, for heaven's sake . . ."

"Stop it," he said, in a low intense voice. "It is for heaven's sake. I don't care what the others do. And I'm not a sissy. I simply want to remain pure. And you must too, Laurence. So if you don't cover yourself decently in future I won't bathe with you at all."

I saw that he was in dead earnest and was wise enough to let the matter drop. We were both rather silent on the way home and I caught myself glancing oddly at him from time to time, but when we got back he stopped, straddled his bicycle, and seemed to want to talk.

"We are still friends, aren't we, Laurie?"

"Of course."

"More than ever in fact. I do wish I was coming with you to Winton instead of being shoved off to Edinburgh."

"Then talk your father into it."

"Oh, no." His face clouded as it usually did at the mention of Dr. Ennis. "I've tried it before. In fact I've often tried, and had no luck, talking him out of shoving me in for medicine. You know, I'd far rather take an arts degree."

I was silent, wondering if some unrecognized or at

least undeclared aversion to his father had put Frank off the idea of medical practice, and with the incident of that afternoon still in mind I said suddenly:

"What surprises me, Frank, is that you haven't plumped for the priesthood. It's so . . . so obvious. Not only would it delight your mother, you're the one person in the world who ought to have a vocation."

He looked at me for a moment then, to my amazement, he burst into a fit of laughter, very boyish and natural.

"You won't have to wait long for the answer to that one, my boy. Next week I want you to meet someone *very* special." Before I could question him he smiled over his shoulder and started to pedal off. "Come on, let's hurry, or we'll miss our half hour with your friend the Canon."

Yes, the impossible had happened, and to Frank's amusement, tinged perhaps with a little chagrin, Dingwall had practically adopted me. One day on the way from school I had come upon a depressing tableau. Frank, frightfully pale, on his knees in the gutter with two of our chief tormentors, the Buchanan brothers, bending over him, the younger of the two holding a can of liquid mud.

"Confess your sins, Ennis, or we'll baptize you with this. Come on, begin: Holy Father I killed a cat . . ."

Intervention, however unpleasant, was the only possible course of action. I snatched the mud can, put the younger Buchanan out of action with a direct hit, then sailed into his big brother. Heavy damage was done on both sides but I had the worst of it and was un-

29

doubtedly due for a bad beating when a sudden apparition obscured the daylight: Dingwall himself, dressed "for the town" with his invariable priestly precision in long black overcoat, black umbrella held upright, and his famous tall top hat, that made him look a mile high. A terrifying spectacle, a veritable specter of Popery, before which, to my gasping relief, even before the umbrella went into action, the Buchanans wilted, and took to their heels.

For a moment the Canon did not speak, then turning to Frank who, still pale, had collapsed against a convenient wall, he said, sadly:

"Go home, my boy, and lie down till you recover."

Then, taking me by the arm, he led me to the presbytery and upstairs to his study. Still in silence he set about repairing me. I had a badly cut lip, a fat ear, and the inevitable black eye, not to speak of skinned knuckles and a fearful hack on the shin where the younger Buchanan, free of mud, had weighed in toward the end.

"Stout lads, these Buchanans," the Canon murmured, engaged with cotton wool and iodine, and still wearing the hat. "Thank God you have some of that same good Scottish blood in you."

When he had finished with me I had to sit down. He gave me a look, went to a cupboard, brought out a thistle-shaped wine glass and a bottle.

"A tablespoonful of this won't hurt you. It is the genuine Glenlivet."

It tasted extremely genuine.

"Well, Carroll," he went on, "you've been dodging

me rather skillfully for some weeks but I'm happy to have made your acquaintance. And in such not unfavorable circumstances, too." He turned on me his smile of infinite charm. "Since we are no longer strangers I invite you to come here, to my study, with your friend Ennis, on every Friday afternoon, after school, to discuss the affairs of the day, literature, even theology. You accept?"

My head was still ringing with that bash on the ear. I accepted.

"Good." He took out his watch. "As I must go to a school board meeting, for which I am already late, may I ask how you intend explaining your present appearance to your grandparents?"

This, indeed, was a problem already worrying me.

"I could tell them I was sticking up for King Robert the first."

"A subtle thought, Carroll. Emerging from the disgraceful Irish in you. But no, we will not demean a noble action with a lie, for which I perceive you have a natural aptitude. I will telephone your grandfather from the board offices."

So that, exactly, was the beginning of my association with a remarkable personality. His objective was not then apparent to me and became so only when it had failed. But for many months I was to enjoy the benefit of his wit, learning, and kindly charm. They left their impact upon me.

Today, however, I was less attentive at our usual session, I kept wondering what Frank had up his sleeve and who might be this someone special.

31

School was on the point of breaking up and on the following Thursday Frank and I set off for home together. He lived at Craig Crescent not far from my grandfather's house, and we took the same road across Levenford Common. This afternoon, however, with an offhand yet mysterious air, he said:

"Let's go by the station tonight. I've someone to meet there."

"Who?"

"Cathy Considine."

"And who's she?"

"She's my girl, Laurence."

I must have shown my amazement. He laughed delightedly.

"We've known each other since we were kids. Brought up together in our prams so to speak. It's not surprising we're in love with one another."

Now I was staggered. All that gush about holy purity and now this . . . this early commitment to Venus. God, you're a queer one, Frank, I thought. And I was suddenly extremely curious to see Cathy Considine.

"She's at the S.H. Convent at Dalcair. Home for the holidays. We'll have a ripping time." Frank ran on excitedly as we climbed the station steps to the upper level. Having exploded his news he was eager to talk. "I'm sure you'll like her . . ."

But the train had just arrived and almost at once Frank cried:

"Cathy! Look, Laurence, there she is!"

A stunningly pretty girl was coming toward us, smiling, and with an answering wave of her arm. She was

not wearing her school uniform but, probably as one
of the older convent girls, had on a natty little navy-
blue reefer jacket with brass buttons, a swinging kilted
skirt and a fetching blue beret tilted slightly to one
side. Never could I forget that first view of Cathy
Considine. She was of medium height, her figure supple and free-moving, her expression full of vivacity
and life. Her eyes were dark, almost black, and sparkling with animation against her warmly colored skin.
She had a short, rather flat undistinguished nose but
her mouth was delicious, large, beautifully shaped with
very red lips, parted now in a wide smile which exposed perfect teeth. Her dark brown hair, hanging
loose from her beret, framed one cheek on which, high
on the cheekbone, was a tiny dark mole. I felt my
heart turn over as she drew near and, barely seeing
me, took both of Frank's hands.

"Cathy."

"Frank."

They stood like this, looking at each other for a long
moment, then she gave me a cool examining look.

"Who is the long-legged Borstal boy disguised in an
academy blazer?"

"Just A. N. Other standing in the background of
this lovesick tableau," I said coldly. "Sorry I haven't
a camera. It's so touching."

Her eyes narrowed.

"I'm glad you like it, because we do."

"Well, while you're drooling over each other, have
you any luggage? If so I'll get it."

"A suitcase. In the guard's van."

I left them together, found her case, then we set out for Craig Crescent. Frank offered to carry the case, which was no lightweight, tried to bring me into the conversation, but without much luck. She was too busy with him, and apparently bent on excluding me. This vacation was going to be the greatest fun. They'd been set a competition at school to see who could bring back the best album of pressed wild flowers. A silver cup was the prize.

"Naturally I'm not wild about botany, Frank. But I'd like to win that cup. Just to put Sister Philomena's eye out, the old hag, she always has her knife in me. And it'll be terrific fun scouring the Overton woods, and the Longcrags too."

Frank agreed with enthusiasm, half turning to me. "You'll join us, Laurie."

"Well . . . possibly," I said, distantly. "If I have time."

"Of course you will. Now, here we are. You'll come in and have tea. Joint invitation from Cathy and me."

"No thanks. I'm expected at Davigan's," I lied calmly and atrociously. I loathed the Davigans, and Daniel the son I particularly despised.

"Well . . ." Frank said doubtfully. "If that's so . . ." The Considine house was next door to Ennis's property, a villa of the same size, with an adjoining unfenced garden which suggested intimate communications. I put the suitcase down at the front gate. Cathy was inspecting me with a critical, not quite comprehending, yet definitely unfriendly eye.

34

"I'm obliged to you, porter. Was it too heavy for your delicate constitution?"

"A mere trifle. What have you inside? Coals or steel corsets?"

"Both, naturally. And a hair shirt. How much is the tip?"

"Pay Frank," I said. "I usually stand in for him when any physical effort is required."

As I took off I saw color flood Frank's face at this underhand reference to the few engagements I had undertaken on his behalf and I felt badly about it. I blamed her, of course, and swore I would have nothing more to do with her. Yet, walking home in a rage, my mind was exasperatingly full of her. When I'd had my tea I put a few deliberately offhand inquiries to my grandmother. Yes, she knew of the girl's mother in a general sort of way. Mrs. Considine was the widow of the late head draftsman at Dennisons, comfortably off on a life pension from the shipyard, a stout, lethargic woman whom I now vaguely recollected moving slowly, bedizened in beaded black, to a front seat in St. Patrick's.

"So you've met her daughter?"

"For the first and last time."

"They say she's rather spoiled."

"She's the giddy limit."

Nevertheless, while I hated this little trollop in the brass-buttoned reefer jacket, I had fallen for her, stricken with the ridiculous anguish of an adolescent first love. When Frank came to the Bruce house next morning, without the slightest reference to my ill humor of the day before, my resolutions broke down, I agreed to go botanizing that afternoon.

Nothing could have been more mistaken, more fatally damaging to my self-esteem. Never before, even in the worst discomfitures of a penurious youth, had I been made to feel so unwanted, not of course by Frank, but by her. Our few verbal exchanges, at first deliberately offensive, became toward the end of the expedition heatedly hurtful, and I swore by my favorite saint—Augustine before his conversion—that I would never go out with them again.

To assist them in their idiotic floral hunt they had roped in and were occasionally accompanied by that other youth, Daniel Davigan, a despicable hanger-on, a clod who, though he had outgrown it by two years, was still at St. Patrick's parochial school, and whose obsequious attempts at friendship I had stiffly discouraged.

This cooption of Davigan in my place was a bitter pill and since it has point later on he must merit a more accurate portrayal. In appearance he was not prepossessing: a flattish face with ill-assorted features, rusty red hair and the blanched skin and pale greenish eyes that often go with such coloring, as if all his pigmentation had been expended on his scrubby brush. Yet it was his manner that offended me, a blend of truculence and ingratiating intimacy with which he sought to advance himself. Doubtless I was prejudiced. Frank, who disliked nobody, was at least prepared to tolerate Dan who, after all, had his social difficulties as the eldest son of a small jobbing builder, a short, hairy, red gorilla of a man lampooned in the town for his feat of propagating sixteen children, eleven of which survived. Once on a rare visit to the Davigan home I had caught a shuddering glimpse of the marital chamber with its huge brassbound bed on which such incessant procreation and parturition had been enacted and which seemed to justify the lines dedicated to Mrs. Davigan, whose maiden name was O'Shane, and generally attributed to Dr. Ennis.

Oh, a terrible life has Bridget O'Shane,
Three minutes' boredom and nine months' pain.
A fortnight's rest then at it again.
Oh, a terrible life has Bridget O'Shane.

This admittedly was a hard thing for Dan to live down and although I grudged him the privilege of accompanying Frank and Cathy he at least served as a kind of watchdog. Indeed I began to want him to be with them, since when he was not and they went alone I suffered most cruelly, not only broodingly picturing them in the most tender intimacies, but hotly and falsely endowing them with every act of sexual abandonment. Indeed, on many of these summer afternoons I hung about the vicinity of Craig Crescent, behind a convenient wall, in the vain hope of observing some evidence of misconduct and throwing it in their faces. Once, unable to restrain myself as they came down from the wood, I stepped out and brazenly accosted them, peering for signs of guilt. Alas, they only looked happy. Cathy certainly was bright-eyed and moistly flushed, diffusing a heady perfume, entirely her own, and gaily excited, full of life and undulant movement, but Frank, calm and undisturbed as ever, wore unmistakably that confounding expression of happy, guileless innocence. I was on the point of turning away when he called out.

"Look what we found today. An absolute rarity. A bee orchid. And by the way, Laurie, I have to go to the rectory tomorrow afternoon. Why don't you take Cathy up the wood."

It seemed the chance of a lifetime to get even with her. While she watched me with a queer expression, half derisive, half expectant, I said:

"Sorry, Frank, I wouldn't be found dead with your Cathy, in or out of the wood." And I walked off.

From the first I had not meant to go, equally convinced that she had not the least intention of keeping the appointment. Nevertheless, at two o'clock on the following afternoon I was drawn irresistibly to that now detested end of Craig Crescent. And as I came round the final bend there she was, perched on the gate leading to Longcrags Wood. Surprise rooted me.

"So you decided to turn up," she said.

I found my breath. "I wanted to see if you would."

"Well, I did. Disappointed?"

"Not particularly."

She laughed. "That's a strange admission from the Bruce heir apparent. I thought you hated me."

"Isn't it the other way round?"

"I ought to be pretty sick of you. Frank's been feeding me your good points until I almost threw up. Did you know it, he thinks you're quite marvelous?"

"Strange delusion, isn't it?"

"I'm beginning to wonder. It does look as if you'd done some remarkably odd sort of things. I mean, for instance, writing that essay just after you came out of jail and winning the bursary . . ."

There was nothing I could say to this, and a silence fell during which she seemed to study me with a scrutiny so unsettling that I said:

"Shall we get a move on with your collecting?"

"Let's just take a walk." She jumped down from the gate. "The truth is I'm sick of all these ghastly ragged robins and bladderworts. And thanks to Frank I have enough to knock out Sister Philomena's false teeth."

"You want to?"

"Frequently."

"What's wrong with her?"

"Oh, just being herself." As we took the path into the wood, she went on: "Always nagging on propriety and that sort of stuff, making us wear shifts when we take a bath and looking me over as if I was going to have a baby." She broke off. "But let's forget her. I get enough of her at school."

For a few moments we walked on in silence under the tall beech trees that fretted the sunlight on the winding green path. The wood was warm and deeply still. I could not believe that I was physically here with her, in this quiet secret place. Perhaps she felt this too for she moved restlessly and suddenly laughed.

"Funny we're doing this! And getting along quite nicely." She gave me a quick side glance. "I really owe you an apology for being so beastly."

"We didn't get off to a very good start, did we?"

"It was my fault being so chippie at the station. I suppose I wanted to impress you."

"You did," I said, with a sudden constriction of my heart. "I thought you were the prettiest girl I'd ever seen in my life."

She actually flushed and kept her eyes down.

"You see, Laurence," she paused awkwardly, unaware of the commotion aroused in me by her use of my first name. "It's just that I'm so bound up in Frank that I sort of resented his being fond of anyone else. But I don't now. If it means anything to you, and I don't suppose it does, I really like you very much." She hesitated, still not looking at me. "I only hope you'll like me."

Now my heart seemed to expand and fill my chest so that I could scarcely breathe. With all the anguish of unsullied adolescence I managed to say:

"If you want to know, I fell in love with you the minute I set eyes on you."

She gave a shaky little laugh. "You can't possibly mean that. But it's nice of you, Laurence. And a relief. I've been upset and sort of jumpy over our misunderstanding. I suppose," she added hurriedly, "because I felt it was upsetting Frank. He's so . . . so scrupulous about everything."

"Yes, he is."

"Do you think . . . perhaps he's a little too much that way?"

"What way?"

"Well . . . sort of strict about little things. Straitlaced. Just think, if you can believe it, all the time he and I have been up here by ourselves in this lovely wood he's never once kissed me. He says we should wait till we're properly engaged."

"If only I'd had his chance."

Had I spoken these words and if so why had she not protested? Now my heart was thudding like a trip-hammer. She was so close to me our arms touched as we moved slowly up the hill, a sudden contact that ran through every nerve in my body. Yet she made no effort to withdraw. Most disturbing of all was the strange sensation of an answering emotion, an emanation that made my senses swim, an outreaching that sought with a nervous excitement for some long frus-trated fulfillment.

"Oh, dear," she almost sighed. "It's so warm. Let's rest a bit. It's dry and lovely here."

She sank down on the grass by some wild azalea bushes. Her face, sunflushed, was turned toward me, her eyes dark and startled. Beside her, I took her hand, the small palm hot and moist. Her fingers closed on mine tightly, so tightly.

My head was swimming, yet some sense of loyalty remained. This was Frank's girl, how could I poach on his preserves? And more; under his influence and the many sessions we had spent in Dingwall's study, I had achieved a commendable state of virtue, even to the point of serving the Canon's Mass when timed for eleven o'clock. Alas, in this re-creation of the original Garden, the serpent was hissing in my ears and at any moment the apple might fall from nowhere into my companion's lap. Indeed, as though in acceptance of this phenomenon, her eyelids slowly drooped. Then, as I bent blindly toward her, there came from below a shout, a series of shouts, almost a hullabaloo, and as we scrambled to our feet, shocked and shaken, a figure appeared threshing through the undergrowth, Davigan, sweating, panting, propitiating, yet somehow suspicious.

"I thought I'd lost you. Met Frank on Chapel Street. Thought I'd come after you and give you a hand."

He stood there, grinning, the oaf, clutching a tuft of something earthy, while we scrambled to our feet.

"And look what I got for you. I don't know what it is but it looks good to me."

Cathy, her eyes downcast and averted, was fearfully pale. My breastbone was thrumming like a drum. I looked at Davigan and his trophy.

"It's a stinking fennel root, you clod. Why don't you eat it."

But nothing would ever get Davigan down. He hung on to us all afternoon and when I could stand it no longer and took off he was still there.

My state of mind may be imagined as I swung across Craig Crescent on the way home. Suddenly at the corner Dr. Ennis came out of the side surgery door, carrying a cased salmon rod and a gaff. He called out.

"How's the gooseberry today?"

Although I couldn't trust myself to speak I forced a sickly smile.

He looked at me keenly.

"Want to come fishing?"

I knew that the good-natured old rip was sorry for me, apparently mooning around at a loose end. To preserve my self-esteem I should have refused his invitation. But I needed companionship and I liked to go fishing. Often I'd gone out with my father before he became ill.

We got into the old black Ford. Dr. Ennis drove in silence and as could be expected, at a wild, erratic speed. We were soon at Malloch on the far side of the Loch where he had a boat, and until late afternoon I sculled hard for him, sweating desire out of me, while he cast across all the likely bays. It looked like being a blank day, but just as we were coming in he changed his fly to a big Zulu and at the first throw was into a fish. Ten minutes later I struck with the gaff and had it in the boat, a fine fresh-run salmon.

"A good twelve pounds." He chuckled. "You did well for me, lad. And with the oaring too. This deserves a drink."

We beached and padlocked the boat, went up the shingle to the bar of the Blairmore Arms where the doctor, after displaying our catch with a good deal of profane boasting, ordered a double John Dewar.

"And what's yours, Laurence?"

"Beer," I said, hardily. I would have died sooner than ask for lemonade.

He laughed. "You'll make a good medical student. Give him a mild bitter, barman."

About an hour and three double whiskies later, Ennis nosed his way into the soft dark night, racked the gears, and we set off for Levenford. I felt cozy after that second order of not so mild ale and the doctor was in high good humor. He liked an audience, and in the bar he had unloaded his repertoire of broad Scots stories on the locals. He kept chuckling, coughing and grunting to himself. Suddenly he said:

"Carroll, you're a lad after my own heart. What's your opinion of this damn business between my son and that Considine girl? It's been going on since they were in their blasted hippins."

"Well, sir," I said carefully. "I think they're extremely fond of one another."

"You mean to tell me they're in love? At their age?"

"They certainly mean to get married when they're a bit older."

"Heavens almighty! But what goes on the now, up in the woods, the two of them, thegither?" He always lapsed into broad Scots when excited.

"Nothing, sir. Absolutely nothing."

"My arse and Jeannie Deans!" He exploded. "They must do something."

"They pick flowers, sir."

"Almighty heavens!" He was silenced. Then: "Listen, lad. That girl drips sex like one of McKay's Ayrshire cows leaks milk. Do you mean to tell me that up in these Longcrags with not a soul to watch them, Frank isn't . . . you know what?"

"I swear to you he isn't. I know Frank. He's good. Absolutely good." With two pints of Tennant's best inside me I felt noble, rising in defense of my best friend. "Why, his influence has even kept me good. He's incapable of anything like that!"

44

"Oh, Lord." He gave out a kind of groan. "You mean he's not trying even for a tickle?"

"Positively not, sir. I'd swear to it."

Again he was silent, then he murmured to himself: "But picking flowers. What a daisy."

We were approaching the lights of Levenford and had reached Craig Crescent before he spoke again.

"Come ben the house and I'll give you your half of the salmon."

"Oh I couldn't, Doctor . . ."

Despite my protests he insisted, giving me the better tail half which sent my grandmother into such transports she didn't even ask to smell my breath. I refrained from telling her the doctor's final remark.

"I daresay ye'll get it served with Bannockburn sauce."

Before I went to bed I said some extra prayers, celebrating my deliverance from the curse of Adam. But all of that night I scarcely slept one hour.

three

DAWN COMES EARLY in the Swiss uplands and on the morning of October 7, although it went against the grain, I was up with the lark to make a quick round of the ward. We had only five cases, none of them serious: two simply retained for observation after pleurisy, a mesenteric adenitis and a synovitis of the knee, the so-called "white swelling," both certainly due to bovine TB, and finally an early Pott's curvature that I had already put in plaster. By half past eight I had finished and after breakfasting and checking with Matron, whom I had already skillfully briefed and who, to my surprise, seemed quite intrigued at the prospect of the new arrivals, I set out for Zurich in the clinic's Opel station wagon. Why so early, Carroll? Why such indecent haste? You are not duty bound to meet and greet the dear pilgrims until half past five. Could it be that there was purpose in that telephone call last night when the good Matron had retired and that once again you are putting pleasure before business?

At first the mountain road is steep, winding and narrow, but beyond Jenez it opens out into the Coire valley. At this hour, except for a few farm wagons, there was no delaying traffic. I made good time and was in Zurich, cruising along the Tielstrasse, looking for an unmetered parking place, just after eleven o'clock.

Zurich has been decried as a city of underground bankers. I have nothing against bankers, since I never meet them, and I liked this fine, rich city, presiding over its broad river and the Zürichsee with the dignity of an elder statesman, and never cluttered with gaping tourists, since most foreigners came quite simply to visit their money. A stroll down the Bahnhofstrasse, where I stopped at Grieder's to buy a couple of ties, brought me to the Baur-au-Lac just before noon. I went into the garden and ordered a dry martini. It came at once, substantial and really dry, with a thin curl of well-pared lemon peel, confirming my unbiased award of five stars to this superb hotel. Naturally it is expensive, but now that I had some sort of income I enjoyed blowing it; moreover my visits were infrequent and as Lotte enjoyed everything deluxe it paid off to indulge her here.

She arrived at that moment, bareheaded and smiling, very smartly turned out in a plain but attractive tan suit that exactly matched her corn-straw hair. I should explain that Lotte is Swedish with the coloring of her race, not the conventional slinky fictional blonde, but a big, easygoing, solidly beautiful girl with the athletic body of a champion discus thrower and careless honey-colored eyes that usually seem full of laughter. Of course she doesn't throw the discus. She is an ex-air hostess promoted to receptionist at Zurich for a big Scandinavian charter line—the Aktiebolaget Svenska Örnflyg—and, both being practiced in the art, we had picked each other up in the airport bar about four months ago when I was dispatching a consignment of boys to Birmingham. I had become fond of Lotte since then and except for one thing I would have been mad about her. As it was, I warmed all over as she sat down and crossed her legs under her short skirt. But the waiter was already at my elbow.

"I'm one ahead of you," I said in German. As part of her job she spoke five languages and, teaching it the best way, had brought my German to what might justly be termed top form—we often laughed together over the way I'd had on the committee with my *"Entschuldigen Sie, mein Herr, können Sie mir zeigen wo das nächste Abort ist?"* "Can you cope with a double?"

"If you'll have one."

I leaned forward when the waiter had gone.

"You're looking most unbearably attractive, darling."

"Thank you, sir."

"Been meeting many V.I.P.'s lately?"

"Lots and lots. Dark handsome men."

"Hmm. African or Burmese?"

"No, no, one Italian, one French."

"Ah! A mixed vermouth."

She laughed shortly, narrowing her cat's eyes.

"Really, I'm serious, Laurence. Two gorgeous men."

49

"Liar. Only don't start sleeping with them or I'll break your Swedish neck. Incidentally," I said, with a momentary anxiety, "you *are* free this afternoon? You weren't quite sure last night when I called you."

"What about those medical researches?"

"We'll work on them together."

She kept me on edge for a moment then nodded, companionably.

"Not on duty till five o'clock."

"That's perfect. I have to be at the airport myself then." And I told her briefly I was meeting a patient and his mother.

The waiter had brought two menu cards with the drinks. We studied them in silence, ordered, and half an hour later we went into the restaurant, a glassed addition built out into the garden with the river on one side.

I remember so well that delicious luncheon, the last before my troubles began. We both had the iced cantaloupe as a starter, so golden, so sweetly ripe, and dead ice-cold. Lotte, who never seemed to look ahead, or perhaps had no need to supercharge her vitality, chose for her main course poached turbot with hollandaise sauce and little new potatoes vapeur. I had a thick filet mignon cooked *au point* with spinach and *pommes pont neuf*. We drank two of the best, yet relatively inexpensive Swiss wines, she the light Döle Johannesburger, I the red Pinot Noir, and just enjoying the food and looking at each other, we didn't talk much. Coffee was all we wanted afterwards, and we put it down suspiciously fast.

Lotte's apartment was in a new block in Kloten, quite near the airport. I drove there, parked the car at the rear of the building and was beside her as she turned the key in the door. I knew it all: living room with small kitchen off, bedroom and nicely tiled bathroom, all furnished simply and functionally in modern Scandinavian style and excessively clean. Whenever we entered she drew the curtains in the bedroom, gave me her big warm smile and began with complete naturalness, keeping her eyes on me, to take off her clothes. Soon she was stretched out flat on the bed.

"Come quick, Laurence. It is too long since the last time . . . I want lots and lots of loving."

Stark naked, lit by the filtered daylight, she invited the physical act openly, naturally and with undisguised desire.

Afterwards, she studied my face, so intense, it seemed to amuse her.

"We must have a cigarette." She rolled over, like a big languid cream-fed yellow cat, reaching to the bedside table, speaking in English which she knew moderately well. "Then again we have much more fun-fun."

That, exactly, was the trouble with Lotte. Bliss when we made love, and afterwards nothing. No tenderness, no persistent sense of belonging, nothing of that yearning which springs not from the body but from the spirit. Of course, an excess of yearning could be dangerous: to my cost I had learned how difficult it could be getting rid of a yearner, particularly the soulful type. But surely, I told myself, there should be *something*, a communication of the heart rather than the adrenals, that endures after the intensity of such a union. Was I asking for the moon? In this case, perhaps. The Swedes, I reflected sadly, were known as prolific copulators, they took it all in their athletic stride. A hygienic exercise.

Lotte drew on her cigarette, her mind already diverted to the mundane.

"Who are these people you are meeting?"

"I told you, darling. A small boy and his mother. It's odd . . . Years ago I fancied I was in love with her. Yet in a queer sort of way I almost hated her."

"See you go on hating. No more of the other thing."

"You can bet on that . . . But Lotte, you don't really love me."

"So you want to be loved? Heart to heart. And pink roses round the door."

"Don't jeer, Lotte. I mean something deeper . . . that you can hold on to when you need it . . . when you're not on top of the world."

She burst out laughing.

"When the dog barks at you in your dark street."

Once, misguidedly, I had tried to confide in her. I was silent. Perhaps she sensed that she had hurt me. She said quickly:

"Ah! Love, what is that but meeting trouble? I like you much. We give each other much satisfaction. And I'm not a gold brick."

"Gold digger," I corrected.

She repeated the words, laughed, then put her arms round me.

"Come. We forget love and enjoy each other."

It was quarter to five when she got up and dressed. With my hands behind my head I watched her out of one eye. In the comedy of life nothing is nicer than a pretty girl stepping out of short, clean white pants—you can keep all your tiddy pastel shades. The reverse process, the stepping in, now being enacted, strikes a bourgeois note. Drawing the curtains, shutting up shop. But in her perfectly fitting saxe uniform, the cockaded bonnet not the common saucy touch but elegant, she looked distressingly smart. The afternoon, which had slightly tarnished me, had put a bloom on her.

"We must hurry, or I'll be late."

I sighed and heaved out of bed. My knees creaked. I was no longer young and healthy.

"I do hate leaving you so soon, Lotte. After being so close to you . . . it's a wrench."

She shook her head.

"You are a nice man, Laurence, of whom I am so fond. I never thought for an Englisher I could feel so much. Don't spoil it all with such sentimism."

"Sentiment," I amended sadly. "And I'm Scottish."

I brought the car round to the front entrance and we drove to Kloten. You may accuse me of being over-sold on Zurich when I commend Kloten Airport as the best in Europe—meticulously efficient, immaculately clean, with a first-class restaurant and a snack bar serving the best coffee I ever drank. We each had a quick cup, standing up. Typically, there was no one at the B.E.A. counter, but from the long range of bustling Swiss desks on the other side Lotte came back with some bad news.

"Your flight is seventy minutes late."

"Oh, blast."

She showed all her lovely teeth in an irritating smile. "You must sit and dream of me, *liebling*. With your so tender heart. And I tell you. When your friends arrive I bring them quickly through customs to you."

I went through to the lower bar, found a quiet corner and ordered a kümmel. Suddenly I felt tired and unaccountably depressed. No, not unaccountably—it was the old post-copulative triste. The Augustine tag came to my mind: *Post coitum omne animal triste est.* How true, how everlastingly true! Usually I can ignore it but today I failed to shake it off. Her crack at my secret hallucination had upset me. And what a fool I was, wasting my time, and substance, in fact wasting my life with these frivolous fringe benefits. Lotte wasn't a bad sort, but what did I really mean to her. A partner in fun-fun. And although she wasn't promiscuous, I had a dismal notion that I was not the only one to share her suspiciously broad and springy bed. But this was the least of my sudden dejection. That mood was coming on, that familiar cursed mood, the epigastric syndrome, or if you prefer it, that psychological punch in the guts. For me there was no escape. Never. Even as a backslider I could not escape that sense of guilt. I had been brought up on sin, both varieties, venial and mortal, the latter, if unforgiven, a prelude to damnation. Ah, goodness, that comprehensive word, that ever-elusive state of good!

Oh, cut it out, Carroll. Be your age. You gave up all that truck years ago. And nowadays who gives it a

54

thought? And if you want to argue, hasn't the recent Commission of Christian Churches practically sanctified all forms of premarital sex, throwing in a few self-service practices as extra jam, with three hearty Christian cheers for *Lady Chatterley's Lover!*

With an effort I turned my thoughts toward the approaching meeting, which disagreeable though it might be, was not without a certain mild expectation. Interesting, in a minor way, to see Cathy again and to know if anything of that juvenile regard for me remained. The probability stirred faint memories and, encouraged by another kümmel and a sustaining club sandwich, I drifted back to Levenford, to that eventful day, and the events leading to it, when I had last seen Cathy Considine and Francis Ennis, the day of Frank's ordination.

four

THE SUMMER THAT YEAR had been exceptionally fine, and on that late August morning as I set out from Winton station the sun beamed benignly in a cloudless sky.

The train was a "local" and as the slow journey wore on with stops at several stations, I had ample time to reflect on the event that was bringing me to Levenford. Actually it was an inconvenience for me to make the trip, since having graduated M.B. at the university during the month before, I had signed on as ship's surgeon in the S.S. *Tasman*, a cargo cum passenger liner plying between Liverpool and Sydney, now due to sail on the evening of the day before the ceremony. But I had promised Frank to be there on his big day, although since leaving Levenford to attend the university my communications with him, to say nothing of my visits, had been infrequent. Frank's sudden decision to enter the priesthood, so logical in one sense, had taken me by surprise. He had never spoken to me of a vocation, although I had long suspected it.

I had already surmised that a subconscious aversion to his father's way of life, while never admitted, perhaps never recognized, had deterred him from continuing the Ennis general practice. But he had meant to be a teacher, and had set out to take his M.A. degree at Edinburgh. And beyond all other considerations his future had been centered on Cathy, their marriage was an understood thing, practically preordained. What could have upset the applecart? A sudden call to give himself to God? Perhaps there had been pressure from the everlasting Dingwall. This I was inclined to doubt, recollecting an incident when the Canon, detaining me after one of our Friday sessions, had caught me by the collar and shaken me till my teeth rattled.

"It's you I want, with your good Protestant blood. What use would Frank be on the parish milk round? Put a rosary in one hand and a lily in the other and you're done with him."

Had some deeper psychological reason inclined him toward celibacy? There was the occasion when, during one of our conversations—I was then a three-year medical student—Frank suddenly exclaimed:

"Isn't it disgusting, Laurence, that the organ of procreation should be the very sewer through which half the impurities of the body are discharged?" And how his expression had frozen when I laughed.

"You'll have to blame that one on the Creator, Frank."

"Not blame, Laurie," he said severely. "It was meant. By omniscient design."

He was an interesting conundrum, still open to speculation! For reasons that were unrevealed, and remained inexplicable, Frank had suddenly slipped out of his commitment to Cathy and taken off for the seminary.

The train was late in arriving, and although I put on speed from the railway station to St. Patrick's, the service had already begun as I slid into an inconspicuous seat beside a pillar. From this retreat I had a clear view of the altar and of the two front rows, where I made out among a number of others, Mrs. Ennis, Cathy, and what looked like the entire extensive range of the Davigan family.

This ceremony is always impressive and I admit it gave me a bit of a turn. The sight of Frank, all in white, prostrate in an attitude of supreme subjection, made me feel a bit of a sickening character. Since I'd cut loose from Levenford I had not infrequently been in the same position for altogether different reasons.

After the final blessing I waited outside, the emerging congregation, which was large, milling round me. Aware that I should not immediately see Frank, I hoped that Mrs. Ennis or Cathy might give me some idea of his arrangements for the day. However, it was Dan Davigan who found me, pumping my hand and patting me on the back with the insufferable presumption of a lifelong boon companion.

"Well met, man. I saw you, had my eye on you, as you slipped in. Why didn't you come forward, proper like, to the place I'd reserved for you? I'm a St. Pat's sidesman now, y'understand, and I throw my weight around. Anyhow, here we are, and I've an invite for you. Celebration repast at the Ennises' home for six o'clock. You'll be there?"

"I'll try."

"Oh, but you must, or Frank'll never forgive you. Sure, your name's never off his lips."

Restively, I looked about me. I still hoped to have a word with Cathy, but she was lost in the crowd or had already gone. I had begun to move away when Davigan exclaimed:

"And now I've a message from the Canon. He wants to see you. In the sacristy. Poor suffering soul, he's a done man, due for retirement to the sisters next month. In you go, I'll wait for you."

There was nothing else for it. I had to go. The old autocrat was in a wheelchair, but still erect, with a book on his knee. His eyes, sunken, but still burning in their sockets, unmistakably alive, took me all in.

"So," he said, when he'd finished looking me over. "I'd a notion to see you before they sent me to the scrap heap." Without taking his eyes off me, he felt for his snuffbox from under his soutane, using his good left hand and, still adeptly, inhaled a pinch. "I perceive that you have slipped, Carroll. Badly. It's written all over you."

I felt the blood rush into my face and neck.

"At least you've still the grace to be ashamed of yourself. I needn't remind you it was you I wanted in there. I worked hard on you too. All those Friday afternoons." He nodded sideways. "But, with that slippery Irish side to you, you got away. However, don't

60

think you'll ever escape. The seed is in you and you'll never get rid of it."

There was a pause. I was grateful that he spared me a cross-examination of my faults, and somehow sad and shamed that I had disappointed him.

"I hope you're feeling better, Canon," I mumbled.

"I'm as well as ever I was, except for the use of one flipper, and good for another ten years. I'll have my eye on you, Carroll."

"I've always appreciated your interest in me, Canon, and all that you did for me."

"Drop the blarney, Carroll. Just let some of our Fridays stick."

Another pause. He took up the book. "As a quasi-literary character, notably an essayist, do you ever read poems?"

I shook my head.

"Well, take this. It's a prize they gave me at Blairs many a year ago. I've marked one poem. It might have been written specially for you."

When I took the book he snapped the snuffbox shut.

"Kneel down, sinner." I had to obey. "I'm going to bless you, Carroll, and it's not only the Lord's will, but mighty appropriate in your case that I have to do so with the wrong hand. For before God, if ever you achieve salvation it'll be the wrong way—by falling in backwards through the side door."

As I left the sacristy, horribly discomposed, I realized I had barely uttered a single coherent word. To recover myself I sat down in the now empty church and opened the book he had given me. *The Poems of*

Francis Thompson. I had never heard of him. His photograph was the frontispiece, an emaciated, self-tortured face with a faint straggle of moustache.

A bookmark indicated the poem toward which my attention had been directed. I looked at the opening lines. I began to read. My mind, full of the recent interview, and the puzzle of Frank and Cathy, was not on the words, but I wanted to get rid of Davigan, so I sat there reading on, without real comprehension, until I came to the end. Absently, I put the book in my pocket, got up slowly, and left the church. And there outside, still waiting for me, was Davigan.

"I never thought you'd be that long. But maybe he wanted to *hear* you. Where are you off to?"

"To visit my grandparents."

"That's my way also. I'll give you a butty along Renton Road."

In subsequent encounters since that memorable interruption in the Longcrags Wood, my dislike for Davigan had not been mitigated, a feeling which, under his habitual ingratiating effusiveness, I sensed he returned with interest. And now, armed with a greater confidence, an exudation of affluence, and cherishing some secret satisfaction that imparted a smirk to his heavy, pallid features, he struck me as even more objectionable. He was got up in a stiff white choker, spongebag trousers and a cutaway coat, the sidesman's outfit, in which he showed people to their places and shoveled up the two collections, but this sartorial elegance was now brought to the verge of the ridiculous by a bowler hat which sat down on his ears, causing

them to protrude. Prejudice, no doubt, made me liken
him to a stage butler in a second-rate farce. I avoided
the gesture with which he attempted to take my arm
as we set off toward Renton Road.

"A heavenly affair," he began. "And what a fine turn-
out. You were a shade late in getting in, Laurence."

Being first-named by Davigan did not lessen my resentment, but I made no protest, except to maintain
silence.

"I noticed you didn't join us all at the altar rails.
You'd see we all took Communion. Oh, I don't doubt
you're in a state of grace all right. I daresay you weren't
fasting. Of course, Dr. Ennis was an absentee. No use
to pretend he was out on a case. He's not really one
of us now, Laurence. No, no, sadly fallen away. Ah,
what a sorrow for the young priest. But the mother,
ah, there was a joyful face, even though the tears were
running down her cheeks. A saint. That's where Francis, I beg his pardon, Father Francis, gets it. His Holiness I mean. They say the Canon hasn't bespoke him
for St. Pat's, but the mother will press for it, I'll be
bound. Though they tell me the young father's not
too glib with the sermons."

A further silence followed, then with a sly side
glance he said:

"And what did you think of Miss Considine, Laurence?"

"Cathy? I thought she looked extremely sad."

"Ah, didn't we all now, more or less. A fine young
man giving up the world for God. But she looked well,
you thought? She's come on, like, in her looks?"

During the Mass I had found myself watching Cathy, thinking that she had altered in some way but that the change, whatever it might be, had given her something that was not there before.

"She's an extremely attractive young woman," I said shortly. "And an interesting one."

"She's all that, and more," he agreed fervently. "Of course, being all in the black for her mother's decease hardly gives her a chance."

"What!" I exclaimed. "Is Mrs. Considine dead?"

"She is that, nonetheless. This couple of months past. And after a long and painful illness, God help the poor soul. May she rest in peace." He tipped the bowler and made the sign of the Cross. "It's hard on Cathy, for you understand . . ." He gave me a look, "the pension died with her, the mother I mean. Still anon, the dear girl has friends, that fine Spanish lace mantilla she had on came from my own mother, just to show you an example."

He had my attention now.

"But what'll Cathy do with herself? Has she a job? She'll have to give up that big house."

"Well, no." He assumed a considering manner which widened his smirk. "She'll not be given notice to quit. You see, Laurence, being in the building trade like, my old man has bought the house. It's a desirable property and may come in handy in the not too distant future."

"Why so?" I asked sharply.

He let the smirk go. Instead he faced me with a defiant yet triumphant grin.

"As a matter of fact, Carroll, you may as well hear it now, sooner nor later. It's not out yet because of the other attraction, the ordination. But when you speak of Miss Considine you're speaking of the future Mrs. Davigan. Cathy and yours truly are engaged to wed."

I stopped short.

"You're joking, Davigan."

"Devil the joke, Carroll." The grin had become a sneer. "We've come up in the world since you and your stuck-up Prot relations looked down your long noses at us. Take a peep up there."

We had reached the end of Renton Road where it branched to Craig Crescent and Woodside Drive. He was pointing to the lower slope of the Longcrags, visible now beyond the Crescent, that wooded hill where the thrushes nested and wild flowers grew, the choice beauty spot of the town, that same wood where Cathy and I had almost found our Eden. Now the wood was razed, and amid the stumps a rash of jerry bungalows was in process of eruption.

"Oh, God, what a bloody mess!"

"That's what you think! Let me tell you, it's the Davigan Building Estate. Our own financial empire! And it's going to make our pile. Put that in your pipe and smoke it, you half-baked snob!"

He left me with that parting shot and after a long speechless inspection of that shameful, hideous vista I made my way slowly to my grandparents at Woodside Avenue.

Here was a different atmosphere. They were quietly

pleased to see me, finally qualified as a doctor, a result atoning in their eyes for my indifferent start in life. They gave me a simple lunch, a kindness I was able to repay by prescribing for the old lady's rheumatoid arthritis. Bruce himself had slowed down, but still haunting the field of Bannockburn in spirit, spent a good hour showing me marked passages in an old parish register he had recently uncovered from a barrow in the Levenford Vennel. My present mood was tolerant of his obsession—it seemed less a prideful mania than an old man's pathetic delusion—yet while I bore with him my mind kept grappling with that incredible situation not half a mile away, in Craig Crescent. Cathy and Davigan . . . it simply couldn't be! I had to get to the bottom of it. Although I was not due at Frank's until six, toward five o'clock I said good-bye to the Bruces and started off by the back road toward the Crescent.

No sign of life was visible in the curtained windows of the Considine house as I came through the front garden, and when I rang the bell there was a longish pause before Cathy appeared, still wearing the black dress that Davigan had deplored. It made her look older, but to my mind, lovelier. How to approach her? It was difficult. I smiled in a friendly manner.

"May I come in? I'm too early for the banquet next door."

She held out her hand without surprise.

"Hello, Laurence. I sort of thought you'd look in."

The parlor was exactly as I had known it during my rare visits in the past, the same formally placed furniture, stiff, polished, and lifeless as the vase of dried-up honesty on the chiffonier. And there was little animation in Cathy as we sat down on hard chairs on opposite sides of that dead room. Her eyes were dull, she looked only half awake. Perhaps she read my mind.

"I was trying for a bit of a nap after one of the tablets Dr. Ennis has been giving me. I don't sleep too well these nights, alone in the house."

"I was sorry to hear about your mother."

"She's better gone. Cancer isn't much fun."

"It must have been hard for her, and for you."

A silence fell between us, stressed by the slow beat of the longcase clock in the hall.

"And now Cathy," I said, trying to speak lightly, "what's all this I hear about your engagement to Davigan?"

"It's no hearsay." She answered at once, as though prepared for the question. "While nothing's settled, Dan wants to marry me."

"And you?"

"I'd be better off married." She said it quite flatly, then after a pause: "Dan's no prize packet but he's been helpful and kind. His parents too. Since Mother died I've been sort of sunk, Laurence. And of course with the pension gone there's nothing but debts. I wouldn't be in this house now if it weren't for the Davigans."

"Cathy, you're not the one to give up. You'll get over this . . . this upset, and find a decent job."

"Such as? I'm not really qualified for anything."

"At least you could try . . . to make a go of your life by yourself."

"By myself?" She gave me a sudden direct glance, then looked away. "You don't really know me, Laurence. Or do you?"

I did, of course, but how could I speak of it. Dimly outlined against the darkening window, her head slightly drooping on her neck, a sad Rosetti profile, there was in her attitude a softness, a sense of mystery and longing, that touched me to the heart. All I could find to say was:

"Things haven't worked out too well for you, Cathy?"

She did not evade the question, yet the readiness of her answer made it sound forced, unreal. A prepared statement.

"You know I'd been saving myself for Frank for years, looking forward . . . waiting, even thinking he'd chuck the seminary. You're a doctor, Laurie. It can't go on, all that repression . . . it's against my nature." She gave me a wan smile. "If I'm to stay respectable it has to be marriage."

I was silent, unconvinced by her apparent frankness, and with a sudden sense of pain and loss, envy too, as I had a distressing vision of her married, and unrestrainedly possessed by the sidesman of St. Pat's. Instinctively, I wanted to comfort her. I came forward and took her hand. I daren't speak of Frank. Yet my sympathy was tainted with a strong carnal curiosity.

"It must have been a great shock when . . ." I broke off.

"When he preferred the Lord to me. Don't deceive yourself, Laurence." She shook her head slowly. "It would never have worked. How can I dress it up nicely for you, my tender young medico? Frank wasn't made for marriage."

She must have seen disbelief in my face. All the straining humiliation of the past came through in her short, pained laugh.

"The very idea of making love was enough to turn his stomach."

"A psychological block. You could have broken it down."

"Useless to try. Why, I'd realized it years ago when we . . ." She caught herself up suddenly, avoiding my eyes. Then she said: "No, no. Frank's better off in the dog collar. So why shouldn't I make do with Davigan?" She gave me a strange inquiring glance. "He's not such a bad sort, he's come up in the world, and at least he'll warm the blanket."

There was a long silence. What did she mean? She had realized years ago? Even half spoken it contradicted and falsified all that labored explanation. She had not released my hand. Her fingers were limp and unresistant. That old beating had started under my ribs again.

"I suppose you know I was wild about you, Cathy? But I always thought you had a down on me."

She looked away, seeming to pick her words carefully.

"Yes, in a way I resented you, Laurie. But it was because you had what I couldn't take from you. Anyhow, isn't that all water under the bridge now?" She paused, with a shadow of her old provoking smile. "We'll not want to start it flowing again?" There was another longer pause, as of waiting, then, as I struggled to find the proper words, she suddenly stood up and switched on the light. "Time's getting on. I'd better be off to tidy up and change my dress. I can't join the celebrations like death at the feast. I'll be with you in a minute."

When she had gone I got up, paced the room, went into the hall, came back to the room, hearing her movements on the floor above only too acutely. All the feeling I'd had for her had risen again, intensified by a most unusual compassion. I longed to go upstairs to console her, but had not the heart or the nerve to chance making a ghastly mistake or to impose myself unwanted upon her, in her present state of mind. And a sense of decency, again unconscious and induced, perhaps, by my encounter with Dingwall that morning, was holding me back. Why should I further complicate her life when already it had become so sadly tangled?

Before I could decide, a step on the stairs made me look up. She was coming down, wearing a white chiffon dress with a red velvet bandeau in her hair. She had put some color on her cheeks and she looked fragile and unlike herself. She took my arm lightly, and with a trace of her natural spirit said:

"Come on. You can lead in the bride. They'll be waiting."

We went next door and into the Ennis living room.

Here, in a well-heated, unventilated atmosphere, the Davigans were already in possession and our appearance together made Dan start suspiciously. He darted a meaning look at his parents: the mother, a big-boned angular woman, her features indelibly seamed with sixteen successive resignations to the laws of nature; the father, short, thick and bandy, with a stupid brick-red face and the look of a sanctimonious ram. Mrs. Ennis, delirious with happiness, was serving drinks, Powers whiskey for the men, a sherry for Mrs. Davigan.

"A great day it is for yourself, Katie," the latter was remarking with an air of repetition, as she accepted her glass. "A great . . . a holy day!"

"The Lord knows it. What'll you have, Laurence, seeing it's an occasion? We're just waiting on Francis. He'll be pleased to see you."

"Is the young father at his orisons?" old Davigan inquired.

I thought at first it was a joke, but he was dead serious, although he'd probably had a few.

"He's at an interview with the Canon."

"Ah . . . the Dingwall himself. It'll be for the curacy."

"You're hoping he'll be lucky, Katie?"

"Oh, yes, dear, I've prayed for it. I would dread a separation."

"Come over and sit by me here, Cathy," said Davigan the younger, after a brief silence.

"I'm all right where I am." She was half seated, half standing by the window ledge. "Is nobody giving me a drink?"

"Of course, dear," Mrs. Ennis said coldly. "You'll have a drop sherry?"

"If you don't mind I'll take the malt. Dr. Ennis prescribed it as a nightcap."

Mrs. Davigan raised her eyebrows.

"Well, well!" she said, in the tone of a future mother-in-law.

"Is the doctor himself likely to be detained at his case?" asked old Davigan meaningly, after a silence.

"He's at his surgery now. And I know he's due on a confinement. But in between he promised to look in."

At that moment there were brisk sounds outside and Frank came in as though he'd been hurrying—smiling, cheerful, radiating such an air of heaven only knows what one could call it, simple, natural or supernatural goodness perhaps, or if one were cynical, priestliness. Yes, Francis was now the ecclesiastic, neatly habited in rows of black buttons, walking on the balls of his feet, smoothly shaved, ready of smile, an idol for the aged parish spinsters. He came directly toward me and took both my hands warmly.

"It's so good to see you, Laurence. Thank you for coming."

Then, to the others: "Sorry I'm late," he apologized. "I had a long session . . . quite a lecture in fact. But I'm to stay, Mother."

Congratulations drowned Mrs. Ennis's ecstatic sigh, and after Frank self-consciously said grace, we sat down to a lavish spread of all that is worst in that destructive Scottish meal which combines tea and supper and is normally served at six o'clock. Mrs. Ennis, a

72

parsimonious housekeeper, had thrown caution to the winds, producing such extremes as boiled silverside and black bun, sausages and trifle, ham, tongue and cherry cake. But for all this variety and the pervading air of pious gaiety which accompanied its dispatch, it was a strained and difficult repast, with undercurrents springing from the circumstances that had brought us together. Of Frank himself there could be no question. Whatever his physical composition, his behavior was perfect: quiet and unassuming, gentle toward his mother, tolerant of the frequent Davigan lapses into bad taste and, beyond an occasional moment in which I detected strain, considerate and affectionate toward Cathy. And suddenly I saw him for what he was: a made-to-order celibate who from his first glimmerings of understanding had been taught, brought up and conditioned to regard chastity, that cardinal virtue of the Church, as the essential objective of his being, whose heart responded fervently to that final dramatic peroration of Canon Dingwall's mission sermon: "Show me a pure man or woman, and I will show you a saint." A belief so self-exaggerated that the mere thought of physical union was gross, repugnant, a defilement to be rejected instantly from his thoughts. Of course he had loved Cathy, but with a total sublimation of sex, an idealized conception of marriage so impractical, if it had not been pathetic, it would have been a joke.

Conscious of my own earthy bondage, I could not help admiring, even half envying, this built-in continence. Yet I felt sorry for Cathy. Her glands had not

73

been presanctified. She had been let down and humiliated and she was hating it, probably hating Frank too, since she remained moodily and unresponsively silent. Had she thought to hurt him by taking Davigan on the rebound? It was a possibility, yet I wondered if she really could go through with it—marry that vulgarian who, lit by a few double Powerses and a final Guinness, which he drank to the trifle, was becoming increasingly possessive. I wanted to tell her: "For your own sake, don't, Cathy," but as she moved restively in her chair, not eating but defiantly pouring herself another drink, I did not have a chance, time was getting on, and having asked myself uncomfortably throughout the meal what the devil I was doing in this galley, I now felt like a fish out of water. I looked at my watch: almost quarter to eight: I must leave soon for my train.

I had hoped to see Dr. Ennis and just as I got up to go his shaggy head came round the door. He was cold sober. He must have made a considerable effort since at this hour he was usually the best part of a bottle to the good. Knowing how he had wanted Frank in the practice, I dreaded a scene. But he was completely in charge of himself, talked civilly and pleasantly, made a few innocuous jokes welcoming me to the profession, then as he went out to his case, he caught Cathy by the arm.

"Come along, dear lass. Time for you to turn in for your good night's rest. I'll see you home. You'll never dance at your own wedding or raise a fine brood of altar boys for Frank if we don't make you a big strong girl."

At the doorway I stepped into the hall to let her pass. She held out her hand.

"Well, good-bye, Laurie, it'll be long enough before I see you again . . . if ever."

"Good-bye, Cathy."

How acutely, painfully conscious of her I was as she stood there, close to me, looking me straight in the eyes. It was a look that lasted longer than it should, filled with a strained anxiety and something else that went direct into my heart. Then she turned away and I watched her go out with the old doctor. After that I had to get away, and despite Frank's pressing me to wait for a later train, I hurriedly said good-bye.

Outside, in the clear dry night I stood, motionless, hearing the vanishing sound of Ennis's Ford, looking at the dark Considine house. A light went on in an upper window, then the blind was drawn. That brought a sigh out of me, not ecstatic like Mrs. Ennis's, just sad, the lament for a lost happiness now gone forever. What was I anyway? An eager Romeo or a jilted lover? Neither. I was a substitute ship's doctor on my way to Australia. With an exclamation that Frank would not have liked, I turned up the collar of my coat, stuck out my chin and set off at a hard pace down the road toward the railway station.

five

A HAND ON MY SHOULDER was shaking me with unnecessary vigor. That, and the roar of a jet taking off, returned me to Zurich Flughafen. I started, turned sharply, and there was Lotte in the airport bar, standing over me with a woman and a small boy beside her.

"You went to sleep . . . again?" With an embarrassing emphasis on the last word, Lotte laughed, put down the suitcase she had been carrying, then said to the others: "You are all right now I have delivered you. But do not trust this man too much, Mrs. Davigan. He is not so simple as he looks."

Cathy muttered some words of thanks. I kept staring at her, in total unbelief, like an idiot. At first sight I had barely recognized her. My mental picture was not more than eight years out of date, but here was a woman who seemed much older, with a strained, almost broken-down look. Her expression was harder, her mouth, though full, was no longer tender, and her eyes, those wonderful dark eyes, had an edgy, questioning look, as though she would find it difficult to smile. She had on a felt hat without much shape and a brown suit, cheap-looking and shabby, but neat enough to do justice to the one thing that was unchanged. Her supple, fluid figure and the natural grace with which she stood and moved had the same appeal that had once made my heart turn over with desire. But now I had no more than a strange and painful awkwardness, pity perhaps.

"I'm afraid you had a bumpy flight," I said, when Lotte had gone. "Can I get you something before we start?"

"I couldn't eat a thing. But," she hesitated, not looking at me, "I'd not say no to a drink."

"Coffee?"

"I'd rather a brandy, if you don't mind."

"What about the boy? A sandwich?"

"He ate some of his dinner on the plane. He's probably too tired to eat."

I bought her a cognac, with a ham sandwich and a Coca-Cola for the boy. He thanked me. Until now he had not spoken, although he had been studying me with observant eyes. He was extremely pale, too slightly built by far, with a reserved, examining expression—a delicate, even gentle look, if it had not been so composed. His brow was the best part of his face, which thinned toward the chin, a feature reminiscent of his father who, I recollected, had a receding jaw. He was wearing gray shorts and stockings and a hand-knitted gray jersey. What was his name again? Of course . . . awful but inevitable . . . it would be Danny boy. Dislike rose up in me, at the memory of Davigan, but I checked it with a false kindness.

"Don't finish your sandwich, Daniel, if you don't want it."

"I'll keep this piece for later." He wrapped half in the waxed paper it had come in.

His mother's silence was so awkward, so restrictive indeed, I had to keep talking to him.

"Your first flight I suppose? It didn't upset you?"

"Oh, no, thank you. I played a game part of the time."

"A game?"

"Yes. Chess."

I smiled, in an effort to lighten the situation.

"Who did you take on? The pilot?"

"He plays games against himself." His mother broke in almost sharply, as though my facetiousness had offended her. "He has a pocket set." After a moment, still in that unnatural and distant manner, she said: "Are we going to Davos or not?"

"Decidedly not. We have everything ready for you at the Maybelle."

"The Maybelle?"

Was there the vague inflection of a gibe?

"Ridiculous name, isn't it? But I think you'll like it."

"Is it far?"

"A longish drive, I'm afraid. We'll leave as soon as you're ready."

When she put down her empty glass we went out to the parking lot. As before, I carried her suitcase.

On this occasion it was light. I sat the boy in the back seat of the car.

"He can stretch out there and perhaps get a sleep."

After a momentary hesitation she got in beside me.

For some time I drove without speaking, taking the bypass to avoid central Zurich, striking the shore of the See beyond, hoping that silence and the darkness might relax her nerves. Any anticipation I had entertained of our meeting, a reunion one might say, born of nostalgic recollection of the past, had been flattened by the stiffness of her attitude. And I had not failed to notice that she kept herself apart, well over to her own side of the car. Had Lotte's remark upset her, as it had me? I made another effort to start the conversation.

"I owe you an apology for not being at the barrier to meet you, Cathy."

"Yes," she said. "If it hadn't been for your girl friend we'd have lost ourselves completely."

My girl friend. So that had nettled her. I smiled in the darkness.

"My only excuse is . . . believe it or not . . . that I was thinking of you. Yes, hanging on in the bar, I got into a daydream of the old days, with Frank and you, lost all sense of the present in the past."

"I've had more to think of than that lately."

"Oh, of course," I said appeasingly. "I didn't know you'd lost Dan until I had Frank's letter. I'm sorry. Was he taken suddenly?"

"Yes, very sudden."

"Too bad," I said, trying to sound sympathetic.

Obviously she didn't want to talk of it, so I curbed my curiosity and said:

"Then you've been worried about your boy. How long has he been . . . let's say . . . off-color?"

"About five weeks. We first noticed the TB gland then."

"Well, don't worry, Cathy. We ought to be able to get him right for you. It's not an uncommon condition in children of his age. Just a bovine TB infection. Not the pulmonary type. We'll not worry him by putting him in the ward. I've arranged with Matron for you both to have the guest chalet. It's very cozy . . . usually reserved for visiting committee members."

"The Matron? Is she nice?"

"Not bad at all, if you take her the right way. Oh, by the by," I hesitated, "I had to work a bit of an angle with her . . . to get you and Daniel in together, and with all the fancy trimmings. You see, normally we're not allowed to take parents. So I established a sort of family relationship, told her you were my cousin. You can disown me if you like."

She did not speak for some time, then she said:

"Still playing about with the truth, Carroll. You were always good at it."

After that, I let it rest. Damn it all, I had only put on the act for her sake, to give her a good start with Matron and to get her the privilege of the committee chalet. I drove on in silence, and at speed, climbing now as we left Zürichsee behind, flashing through the villages of Landquart and Jenez, almost deserted at this hour. The night darkness was deepened by the overhanging mountains. There was no mist but a fine rain had begun to fall. I switched on the radio to get the late news and weather report. Another level-crossing accident. Two killed in Grisons. Disarmament Conference reconvened in Geneva. More trouble in the Yemen. Servette had beaten Lucerne in the Cup two goals to one. Brighter weather lay ahead.

From the swift occasional glare as we passed an il-luminated sign I saw that she was sitting erect with closed eyes. Daniel, in the back seat, had fallen asleep, his audible breathing synchronized with the regular beat of the windscreen wipers. I switched on the heater. Out of sheer decency and good-heartedness I had tried to make it a cozy threesome in the snug little Opel, but something had gone sour and it was making the journey twice as long.

However, toward eleven o'clock we were there at last, and as we came up the drive it was a relief to see lights in the guest chalet. I had been a trifle uncertain of Matron, but she had actually stayed up, well be-yond her usual hour of retiring, to make a welcoming party of one.

"Ach, zo! You are tired. Zo late, and zo much jour-neyings." With an arm round Cathy she helped her from the car. "And the leetle boy? Sleeping. That is goot. But zo pale. Can you take him, Herr Doktor? Ve are all prepared."

Inside, the chalet glowed, a bright fire in the little sitting room warmly burnishing the freshly polished furniture, gilding the pot of white cyclamen that since morning had undoubtedly found its way from the village *Blumengeschäft* to the center table. Nearby, on a tray, was a thermos jug flanked by a plate of pretzels. A clean warm smell of burning pinewood seeped from the burning logs. Shaded lights were on in the large and adjoining small bedrooms, both beds were turned down, and on each, light as swansdown, lay that unique provider of nocturnal comfort, a Swiss Steppdecke.

What a tribute to myself that Matron had put herself to such trouble to achieve so warm and convincing a welcome. Cathy, tired and exhausted to the point, almost, of an estrangement with me, looking about her with an expression of dazed surprise, had clearly expected nothing so attractive, so heartwarming.

"You like, *ja?*" Matron said, in a pleased tone, studying her.

"It's perfect . . . so lovely . . . and comfortable. I . . . I don't know how to thank you."

"Goot! Now you must take your hot trink vile I put to bed the child. And for you, Herr Doktor, there is also hot milk and pretzels already in your room. So, *gute Nacht.*"

She bustled through the main bedroom into the little room where I had taken Daniel. As Cathy stood motionless and silent, her eyes lowered, I unstoppered the thermos and poured a glass of milk which I slid along the table toward her. I scarcely knew what to say, exactly what note to strike, how in fact to break the ice which seemed to have formed between us. But it was she who spoke first. Apparently still thinking of Matron she said, almost to herself:

"That's a kind-hearted woman."

"She is, Cathy," I endorsed heartily, then with some justification, feeling that I might take my fair share of the credit, I added: "We both felt, she and I, that you deserved the best."

"Because I was your cousin?"

"Well," I shrugged, "that was just to help things along."

She did not answer but remained, with head averted, not looking at me. At the sight of that drooping figure, still slender, even youthful, another touch of pity came at me. Not the journey alone, trying though that might have been, but some other, harrowing experience, anxiety for the brat, perhaps, I couldn't yet discover the hidden cause, but whatever it might be, it had worn her down.

"Don't worry, Cathy. We'll get the boy right, and you too. I'll examine him first thing tomorrow, and do everything I can to help you."

I came toward her and took her gently, soothingly, by the arm.

Instantly she froze. In a low but intense voice, looking me dead in the eyes, she said:

"Keep your dirty fingers off me. You . . . you lying woman chaser."

I was staggered. After all I had done; inviting her to stay; meeting her; driving her in the pitch dark for hours over these damn dangerous mountain roads; to be blasted like some bloody sex maniac. Then I saw that she was more upset than I, and at once everything became clear. Not just her seeing Lotte, of course, the

big Swede had given me away, yes, all the way—I
might have known she couldn't be trusted to keep her
mouth shut—and Cathy, eagerly looking forward to
meeting me again, had been hurt. Well, it would pass.
I would soon put things right. Meantime, take no of-
fense, remain calm and sympathetic, time would heal
the breach. I said gently, but in a slightly injured
voice:

"I can see you're tired, Cathy. So I'll just say good-
night. I hope you sleep well."

I went out on the balls of my toes, just like Frank,
and quietly closed the door.

six

NEXT MORNING, after my exertions on the previous day, I slept late. After I'd had my croissants and coffee, which was always kept hot in a thermos jug in the sitting room, I ambled into the office. Matron, at her desk, looked meaningly at the clock as I gave her *"Guten Morgen,"* but she was in a smashing good mood.

"Ach, Herr Doktor," she beamed all over her face, "I like much your cousin Caterina. *Ja,* already she asks me to call her so. And she is risen so early, all dressed, and knowing my absence of staff, is helping much with my verk."

"I'm so glad, Matron." Slightly bewildered, I managed to get this out.

"I, also. That is a most goot, nice voman."

These superlatives caught me unawares, but I kept on my smile.

"Where is she now?"

"In the *Küche,* so do not disturb." She raised a minatory finger then nodded with an approving chuckle. "She makes for *Mittagessen* a Scotsman's food . . . the meence."

Hell mend the old battle-ax, she killed me with her mangled double jargon and whatever might lie behind it. But I was still a bit slack-headed myself—I usually felt that way after an outing, or should I say an innings, with Lotte, and besides I'd had all the fag of that late night drive—so I could only beam back.

"I'll leave her to it then. I'm terribly pleased you're friends already. Now I'll go over before my ward round and see the boy."

I walked slowly to the guest chalet wondering what the devil this Caterina was up to. Making a play for Hulda's good will? Could be: to prolong her stay. Or, after years of Davigan, was she just the thoroughly browbeaten domesticated little housewife? *The meence!* It would make a horse laugh.

I opened the chalet door expecting to find the kid in bed, but like his nice goot ma he was up, dressed in his shorts and jersey, bent over an absurd little checkered board on the living room table.

"Good morning." I put into it the usual affability I use for all the kids. "Are you receiving visitors, Daniel?"

He looked up and smiled. "Come into the lion's den."

It seemed a neat sort of remark for his age, but probably someone had at one time tagged it onto him.

"What are you doing?"

"Oh, just working out something."

"You like chess?" I asked curiously.

"Yes."

"Do you always play with yourself?"

"Oh, no. Only when I'm thinking out a problem. At home I play with the Canon."

"Dingwall?"

He nodded.

"Are his old bones still hanging together?"

"Very much so, though he's with the sisters now at the convent and doesn't get about much. He likes a game . . . usually after Benediction. He was the one first put me on to it."

"I expect he licked the pants off you."

He looked up at me sideways.

"When Greek meets Greek," he said.

The remark silenced me. Frank's letter had not erred. This little runt really had something rather out of the ordinary, but I fancied he knew it, which made me want to take him down.

"I'll give you a game sometime. There's a decent full-sized board in the playroom."

"Oh, good. Do you play much?"

"Well, off and on, so to speak," I temporized. "As a matter of fact, there's a café in the village where you can always get a first-class game."

"How splendid. I'd like that. Can we now?"

"Later, young fellow. We've got to have a proper look at you first."

He got up at once and I took him round the main house to the small dispensary that adjoined the ward. He was nervous and tried not to show it, but kept stealing glances at the instrument cabinet and the rows of reagents on the test bench. I felt that Matron had been wise putting him with his mother in the chalet and not in the ward. Stripped to the waist there wasn't much of him. Precious little, in fact, no credit to his late departed sire. Still, most of the kids that came to us were like that, pinched little city sparrows, so almost automatically, or perhaps because I wanted no reproaches from the Caterina, I went over him with extra care: lungs, heart, joints: I gave him a good half hour. In fact, as I put away my stethoscope, he said:

"You took longer than Dr. Moore."

"He's your doctor?"

"He's Dr. Ennis's assistant. At present anyway. He's leaving for Canada."

Another one, I thought, trying to escape from that damned nationalized medicine.

"How is Dr. Ennis?"

"Quite well . . . I think." He looked away. "At least, sometimes."

"I see."

He was still lying on the couch and I bent over and took another look at the slightly swollen cervical gland. Apart from that fairly common manifestation of TB in children, I had not found anything, certainly nothing in the least degree serious. But I wanted to make sure. A well-equipped radiography room opened off the dispensary. Ample funds at the disposition of the Maybelle Trust had ensured that this essential diagnostic unit was completely up to date. Of course, as a rule most of the kids were scared to death of it, so I prepared him as casually as I could.

"You don't mind if we go next door and take a picture of your ribs?"

"X-ray?" he said quickly.

"Nothing to alarm you."

"Oh, I'm not alarmed, Dr. Laurence." He added quickly: "May I call you that?"

Trying to play it brave, I thought, and making a play with first names. I gave no answer.

We went in, and after drawing the heavy curtains I screened him thoroughly. He blinked and turned pale as the current sparked on but beyond that kept perfectly still, and when it was over he said:

"That was a very interesting experience."

I gave him a hard look: I didn't at all go for this precocious, Little Lord Fauntleroy line of talk.

"What should interest you is that there isn't a single spot on either of your lungs. They're absolutely clear."

"I'm not surprised," he said mildly. "I understand that what I'm suffering from is the King's evil. You know," he added: "Scrofula."

"Who put you on to that medieval rot?" I said sharply.

"My friend the Canon. We discussed it during a chess session. And I suppose it is rot. We were inclined to doubt the efficacy of the royal touch . . . as a cure."

What could you do with that, except give him another hard look. He was beginning to annoy me.

"Your cure will be to obey my orders. And for pity's sake stop sounding off as if you'd just swallowed the

Children's Encyclopedia, or I'll begin to think you're just a little toad."

His face fell. I had hurt him, but he tried to smile.

"Couldn't you make it a tadpole . . . that sounds nicer? And I haven't *swallowed* the Children's Encyclopedia, I've only read it once. I'm sorry, Dr. Laurence, I can't help being brainy, it's a bit of a curse, but in spite of it I hope you can put up with me. You see, although I didn't like you at first, I'm rather inclined to like you now."

Good Lord, what was he giving me? But I had to know.

"Why didn't you like me at first?"

"When I saw that the rude Swedish hostess was your girl friend."

That seemed to me enough for one session.

"Get dressed," I said, and began to write up his case history. He was cahectic and underweight, but that would be taken care of, and the gland was not painful or in any way adherent. No point in keeping him in bed. I would do a von Pirquet and watch his temperature.

"Just a minute. Roll up your sleeve. I'm going to make a little scratch on your arm."

"Is that the treatment?" he inquired anxiously.

"No, a test. Your treatment is lots of fresh air, gallons of milk, plenty to eat, and obligatory rest periods after lunch."

When I had finished with him it was almost noon, and I had just time to do my routine ward visit before lunch. The Swiss take *Mittagessen* early, and as this is the main meal of the day, Matron and I always had it together. Today, laid for four, with a big pot of African violets, that specialty of Swiss florists, as a centerpiece, the table had an unusually festive air. Cathy, dressed in a plain blouse and skirt, was already there and after I had said a pleasant word to her I did not fail to compliment the old dragon.

"*Ja*, it is goot to have *gästes*." She smiled at the female guest, who sat with a quiet humility on her right. "Ven ve are without the child-ern ve are so much alone."

Hmm! She hadn't objected to being alone with me before.

As we began on the thick, vegetable, deliciously cheesy soup, I said:

"You'll be relieved, I'm not too unhappy about your boy, Cathy. We'll get him right for you."

"Ach, that is goot, Herr Doktor. But your cousin also needs your care. She tells me this morning of much suffering from her huspand's loss and other bad chances. She must surely stay, also with Dan-iel, till she is better, yes?"

"Oh, of course," I agreed, choking on a spoonful. "Most welcome."

Cathy raised her eyes toward Matron, then lowered them.

"Only if you'll let me help you."

"*Jawohl, meine Caterina*." She leaned over to execute a little arm-patting. "*Aber nur ein wenig*."

Well, well, I thought, there's certainly been some fast work by Caterina in the kitchen this morning—

a deduction fully endorsed when the next course appeared, borne in by Rosa the maid, as though it were a flaming boar's head. After some quite professional tasting, rolling a large spoonful around her double dentures and smacking her lips, Matron leaned back in her chair and clapped her hands.

"*Wunderbar, Caterina!* It is so goot, your meence."

"I'll make it any time you wish," Cathy said modestly. "It's very nourishing, and inexpensive."

"It is like," Matron rolled another full forkful down the hatch, ". . . like a goulash, a ragout."

"My Dan was very fond of it."

"Ach, so, the poor huspand."

"You like it, Cousin Laurence?" For the first time since her arrival she gave me a direct look, blank, yet just possibly one quarter satirical.

"Best Scotsman's meence I ever tasted."

After a short silence, encouraged by that glance, though I did not at all care for the cousinly appellation, I said:

"Perhaps you'd like a short run in the station wagon this afternoon. Get the hang of the countryside."

"No thank you." She refused instantly. "Matron thinks I ought to rest this afternoon."

"*Ja*, is besser to rest," Matron agreed. "After the journeyings."

"But why don't you take Daniel? You'd like that wouldn't you, Danny?"

"Oh, enormously."

"Daniel must lie down too," I said firmly. "I'm going

94

to stretch him out on the balcony, all wrapped up like an Egyptian mummy."

"But ven he arises?" Matron persisted.

I was on the point of saying "no" when I realized that I must for the moment swim with the tide.

"Well, we'll see," I grunted.

seven

IF THE FACT is not already evident I wish firmly to
establish that I have no addiction whatsoever to children. During our "health walks" when two by two the
little blighters make a dismal procession struggling up
the hills in the rain, their thin transparent plastic capes
flapping around their bare skinny knees, peering into
the cow barns, grabbing an occasional common wild
sorrel and shouting "Idlewise," stopping to piddle or
have their noses blown, or to show me blisters on their
heels, then bursting into shrill sporadic song, well, I'll
admit to a shade of what might be called compunction.
For the sake of my job, too, I have to make a show of
interest and sympathy, even a heartiness so foreign to
my nature that it almost makes me puke. So do not
accuse me of more than a grudging effort to fulfill an
obligation when I state that at three o'clock, after I
had written my monthly report for the committee, I
went up to the balcony where I had planked the Davi-

97

gan offspring, quite prepared to take him for a drive. He was awake.

"Have you come to unwrap the mummy?" He smiled.

"You didn't sleep?"

He shook his head. "After your remark at lunch I've been pretending I was one of the Pharaohs and that you'd have to dig me out of the tomb."

"What did it feel like?"

"Very cold." He broke into a fit of laughter and gave me his hand. It was half frozen. The *bise* had risen and I hadn't covered him well enough.

"Why didn't you call out for more blankets?"

"I can't speak Egyptian."

This was going to kill me.

"Never mind," I said. "We'll walk to the village and I'll buy you a hot drink."

On the way down, having been landed with this chore, I felt I might legitimately turn it to advantage.

"Daniel," I said chummily. "It's so long since I've been in Levenford. Is the Davigan Housing Estate still going strong?"

"Oh, yes. Extremely strong." He gave me his upward sideways look. "But not for the Davigans."

"Why not?" I asked quickly.

"Didn't you know? It's ancient history. Grandpa Davigan failed and went bankrupt."

"I can't believe it."

"Only too true, unfortunately. The bank called in the big lot of money he'd borrowed. Before the houses were finished. It was a fearful mess. Everything was lost."

"Good heavens, Daniel!" I exclaimed, masking my satisfaction, drawing him out more. "But surely your father . . . before he got ill . . . I mean, wasn't he connected with the estate?"

"He was employed there by the new owners. But only as a working mason."

I had no need to pretend surprise. I was astounded. Admittedly old Davigan was bone stupid, but he was crafty and he had known his job. Obviously he had got out of his depth and been swallowed by some bigger fish.

"Hard luck, Daniel."

"Hard up, you mean." He spoke philosophically. "That's what the boys shout after me at school. But at least there'll be no more chewing the fat over it at home now Father isn't there. That was never-ending."

"Was your father's a sudden illness, Daniel?" I inquired tactfully.

He seemed to shrink under the question, but glanced up again, this time sharply.

"It wasn't an illness. He was killed . . . An accident. But would you mind, Dr. Laurence, if we don't talk any more about this . . . it upsets me even to think of it."

I scarcely knew where to look, suddenly feeling guilty and ashamed. What a mean, underhand, dirty hound, sneaking information out of him. Although I was eaten up with curiosity, I said hurriedly:

"We'll say no more about it, Daniel." Adding, although I did not mean it: "Never again."

By this time we were approaching Schlewald Platz and, picking up, he began to look about him as we came along the riverbank below the telepheric, crossed the bridge and came into the lower part of the village, which is mostly seventeenth-century Swiss and decidedly attractive. I could see that he liked it.

Outside Edelmann's I took his arm. It was thin as a chicken bone.

"This is where we go in."

As we entered he asked:

"Is this the chess café?"

"No. But it's one where the cakes are a lot better."

Edelmann's, in fact, was known all over Switzerland.

His expression had cleared further at the sight of the superb display of patisserie in the long glass case beside the counter, and when I said "We each pick up one of these plates by the window, go over and stand at the counter and choose," he actually laughed.

"We're a couple of Mad Hatters."

"We're *what* . . . ?"

"Don't you remember, in Alice? He always carried an empty plate about with him in case someone offered him a cake."

When we were seated he ate his cream sponge slowly, as if it were a new experience, savoring each small bite, and washing it down with the hot chocolate I had ordered for us both. When he had finished he remarked thoughtfully:

"That is the best cake I have ever tasted in my entire life. Perfect ambrosia."

"It's the best I've ever tasted, and I've lived considerably longer than you. Have another go of ambrosia?"

"I should imagine they're very expensive."

"We can stand it, this once."

"No, I think not. But perhaps you'll ask me another time, if you feel like it."

Where had the kid got them, among the Davigan ruins—good manners? Cathy, perhaps, if so one good mark to her. Yet more probably they came from the old man in the wheelchair.

When we left I picked up my *Daily Telegraph* at the station bookstall where Gina, the girl there, regularly kept it for me. She was a dark-haired Italian, rather short in the gams but, with her black eyes and white teeth sporting a dazzling smile, chock-full of brio. Although she wore a wedding ring there were no signs of a husband, which made her an interesting prospect. We had made quite a bit of progress already, and while the kid stood waiting, we traded a few repartees.

On the way home I took the main road to make easier walking for him. Suddenly he drew up.

"That's a very striking little church, Dr. Laurence. Is it ours?"

I nodded.

It was one of those small ultramodern R.C. churches that had begun to sprout in Switzerland, part of the new movement to be with it. All lopsided angles of wood, glass and concrete, half imitation Frank Lloyd

Wright and half pure Disneyland, it stuck up in the old village like a sore thumb. Outside, on something like a gibbet, a peal of bells hung off-center. Inside it was naked stone, cold enough in winter to freeze the knackers off you.

You'll gather I could not stand the place. In fact, I hated it. Since I had to take the Catholic children there on Sundays, on more than one occasion it had for various reasons really got me down. Usually, when I had parked them, I'd go out for a smoke, or amble down to the station kiosk to pass the time of day with Gina, who was always open on Sundays, selling soft drinks and cigarettes to the peasants who invaded Schlewald on their one free day.

"It grows on you. I like it." He had completed his survey. "Let's go in."

This was too much—I shut him up.

"You've had enough for one afternoon. We'd better get back."

He was short of breath coming up the hill, stopping now and then to, as he put it, "catch his puff," and to say:

"I have enjoyed myself, thank you, Dr. Laurence."

"Good," I said shortly. I didn't want slop of any kind. "I'm going to take your temperature when we get in."

I saw that I would have to keep a stricter eye on him. And at least further excursions of this nature were out. He was all brains and bumph, and not much else.

102

eight

EVER SINCE that opening luncheon a vague premonition of impending trouble had existed at the back of my mind, but I could never have believed it would hit me so soon. The profound observation of Confucius, that after three days guests and fish stink, was working in reverse at the Maybelle Clinic. By the end of the week it was I, apparently, who seemed slightly tainted while Caterina, as the Matron had rechristened her, was presumably smelling like the rose.

Pondering the matter, in an effort to get to the roots of it as I sat at breakfast in my room, I assembled the evidence, tenuous perhaps and circumstantial, but nonetheless disturbing. My coffee, for instance, was not entirely hot this morning, and on my tray lay not the usual three fresh, tender croissants, but instead a single one, unfresh, and two of those unmentionable *ballons*, the lowest and most debased forms of Swiss rolls, guaranteed tooth-breakers, regular hockey balls. Perhaps the baker's girl, a red-cheeked fräulein who delivered before school, had failed to materialize. I doubted it—she was regular as a Swiss clock, not the cuckoo variety sold to tourists, but a reliable Patek-Philippe. No, as other kindred deprivations came to mind, I found it impossible to evade the suspicion that Hulda had cooled toward me. Definitely tempered was her lush and overflowing affection. A critical glint had invaded her eye, a short laugh now replaced the beaming "ach so" assent that had hitherto welcomed my most speculative observations. At our midday dinner an optical collusion had developed between her new protégée and herself, meaning glances that passed over my head but which I suspected were derogatory to myself, followed usually by remarks exchanged in undertones. On several occasions these had touched with unpleasant significance on my Levenford antecedents in a manner scarcely in accordance with my previous elaborations on this theme. How otherwise regard this little tidbit of a tête-à-tête, which took place in Matron's room just loud enough for me to overhear in the test room next door:

"Of this Scots town of your birth, dear Caterina, you speak seriously? It is not nice?"

"Far from nice."

"But before I am believing it is fine, historique, eine noble *Stadt?*"

"Who could have told you such an untruth? It's a small, ugly, working-class, shipyard town. All day you hear nothing but hammering of rivets."

"But surely . . . I am confuse . . . surely there is a fine castle, on the river?"

"That's just a tumbledown old ruin by a dirty stream."

"No one still lives therein?"

"Only the rats."

"Ach, so! And the peoples are not *hochgeboren?*"

"No. Of course, some think they are."

Hulda's voice, which had risen in tone, octave by octave, in a crescendo of forced amazement, now dissolved in a fit of laughter. Then, wiping her eyes:

"Here, in *der Schweiz,* if some silly Scotsman believes he is *ein König,* he must be put straight away in *Krankenhaus.*"

Equally disturbing was the Matron's remark on the following morning when Lotte, disregarding my injunction never to telephone me, had rung up to say she had an unexpected free day. I couldn't blame the big stupid Swede since at another time I would gladly have joined her in Zurich. But it was Hulda who took the call and afterwards, in a tone impossible to mistake, she had inquired:

"Your professor from the Zürich Kantonspital, Herr Doktor?"

Well, what of it! I was still the boss. Yet when I thought on the instigator of all these scheming little tricks, these dropped hints and innuendos, I felt like wringing her neck or, better still, setting up a good rough bedroom scene with her. What the devil was she after? Beyond the recognition of that strain of antagonism which had always existed in our complex relationship, especially in our early days when she had tried to get the better of me, I could not even guess.

Seeing her every day, in the same house, made it worse. Recovered from the journey, refreshed by the mountain air, she had shed a few years, lost that beaten look, and in the words of that murky ballad, begun to bloom again.

There was a knock at the door.

"Come in!" I shouted.

Daniel's head appeared inquiringly round the lintel. He smiled.

"Are you busy, Dr. Laurence?"

"I'm busy trying to get enough calories out of this bloody bad breakfast."

"It doesn't look too bad."

He advanced and sat down. He was still in his Maybelle dressing gown and pajamas, holding his infernal pocket chessboard.

"It's just that Mother and Matron have gone shopping in the car. I was wondering if, since we were alone . . . we might try a few moves."

So they had paired off again. I glared at him.

"I believe I told you to stay in bed until I came to examine you."

"Well . . . I had to get up."

"What for? To piss?"

"No," he said, adopting my vocabulary. "To puke."

"You were sick?"

"I only threw up a little. It's a bit of a habit I seem to have developed."

"Since when?"

"Just the last few days. I think it's the codliver oil. What comes up all tastes of it."

I looked at him and nodded.

"That's probable. It's pretty foul stuff. We'll knock you off it and put you on extra milk. Now back to your room."

"Won't you? I'm rather tired of playing against myself."

I finished my tepid coffee and pushed the tray aside leaving the *ballons* conspicuously untouched.

"Come on then. I'll give you a game. Then you must come to the dispensary and have your injection."

"Good," he said. "It's a deal," and began to set out the board.

Although I was no Capablanca I played chess off and on with the kids during wet recreation hours, and I meant to knock him off quickly, partly to take him down, but also to eliminate the nuisance of further games.

We began calmly. I had the first move. But why make a song about it. There is no disguising the sordid facts. This unnatural little upstart mated me in exactly six moves.

"That's extraordinary." He smiled. "I never knew the Giuoco Piano opening to succeed so easily. I fully expected you to use Captain Evans' gambit."

"You did?" I said sourly. "Well, I don't go for Evans. Suppose you play me another without your queen."

"Certainly. In that case you'll probably open with the Ruy Lopez."

"Not on your life. I'm anti-Portuguese."

"Oh, Lopez was a Spaniard, in the sixteenth century, Dr. Laurence. He invented his attack—where caution and safety are essential on the defender's part. And I'm sure you'll remember to respond with P to K4."

"That impertinent remark costs you another three pieces," I said, removing his two bishops and a castle. Now I'll give you and Evans a damn good licking."

Even so it was no use. I was cautious but not safe. When he looked at me reproachfully, sparing my feelings by not saying "checkmate," I scattered the pieces back into the box and stood up.

"I'm used to playing with experts: when I'm up against a beginner it throws me off balance."

He laughed dutifully.

"You're just a little out of practice, Dr. Laurence," he said apologetically, following me into the dispensary.

"Don't hand me that eyewash."

I gave him his injection—I had put him on a course of colloidal iron—then told him to go and get dressed. In the office I had some paper work to get through but I could not settle to it. My thoughts were depressingly clouded by the campaign that almost certainly had come into being against me. Before this went further, counteraction, I clearly perceived, was demanded of me.

The ladies, if I may use the word, returned in excellent spirits and a continued sense of intimacy which persisted during the midday meal. Once or twice I caught Matron's button eyes upon me with an admixture of inquiry and that sly glint of jocular malice which, in the Swiss, passes for humor. But as I had wisely decided to say nothing, the expectation that I would complain about the breakfast was frustrated. This at least afforded me a minor satisfaction and for the rest I maintained an attitude of quiet dignity, reserve and, let me add, determination. I had fully made up my mind to have things out with the soidisant Caterina.

She had the habit now of walking after the *Mittagessen*, taking the uphill path beside the little stream that tore down through the pasture with picturesque abandon, between banks of meadow sweet and celandine. Today she did not disappoint me. After she set off, I established Daniel on the terrace and followed her with such discretion that she remained unaware of me until she had actually seated herself on the grassy hillock that marked the end of the lower slopes before the mountain took over in a steep glissade of scree. Beyond, the massed pines climbed darkly into a rarefied world of their own.

"You've discovered a favorite spot of mine," I said, companionably.

She looked up, without surprise or any sign of welcome.

"I suppose you've noticed the heather . . ." I had to keep talking, "not the usual Swiss erica, real Scottish moorland heath. And there's lots of harebells among the bracken."

"Quite like home sweet home for you," she said. "Should it remind me of our happy days together?"

"Well, it ought to arouse your botanical instincts."

"I've lost all my instincts."

Her response wasn't encouraging but I maintained my air of sweetness and light.

"May I join you?"

"Why not? I half expected you."

I parked myself on the short heathery turf. Glancing sideways surreptitiously I had a sudden warm appreciation of the change wrought in her by Alpine air and the Maybelle cuisine. Bareheaded, in a simple Swiss blouse and dirndl skirt which I strongly suspected Matron had bought her that morning, she looked younger and, this came to me with a start, definitely bedworthy. But enough! After a pause of recollection, in a tone which combined both conciliation and reproach, I began:

"It's true, I've been hoping for an opportunity to talk with you. I've had the strangest and most unnatural feeling that in spite of all I've done and intend doing for you and your boy you've . . . well . . . turned dead set against me."

"I have. And I am."

The brief reply, delivered without emotion, shook me.

"For heaven's sake why?"

She turned slowly and examined me.

"Quite apart from your character, Carroll, which is unspeakably and sickeningly detestable, you've always been a sort of evil genius for me. Yes, from the day I first saw you on that railway platform. If you want it in a few sloppy words, I'd say you have botched up my life."

Speechless, I could do no more than gape at her. She went on.

"I never thought I'd have the chance to even the score. Now I have."

Was she out of her mind? I struggled to find words.

"But Cathy . . . how can you . . . it's inconceivable that I should want to injure you. I've always been fond of you and I have every reason to believe that you . . ."

"Yes, at first sight, on Levenford station, I had the misfortune to fall for you, head over heels. And I couldn't shake it off. It was you broke up my attachment to Frank. I might have had him if I had tried. I didn't try. You were always on my mind. I wanted you. I was sure you would come back when you graduated. Well, you did. And then . . ."

"You were engaged to Davigan."

"Never. That was just a phase of weakness. I would never have married him," she paused to achieve a more deadly effect, "if you hadn't sneaked off like a rat at six that morning before I was awake."

So it was out, as I had feared. She had hit the nail on the head. There was a long and for me an uneasy silence. I pulled myself together, cleared my throat. I meant to speak soulfully and in the circumstances the throb in my voice came almost naturally.

"Cathy," I said, trying to make it ring true, "I hope we're not going to desecrate what was, at least for me, the most wonderfully memorable experience of my life. When we said good-bye after that ghastly celebration for Frank's ordination you must have sensed how much I needed you and how much, thinking of

111

your attachment to Davigan, I was fighting it. As you know, I set out for my train but had, simply had, to turn back to you. I won't embarrass you, now, by dwelling on the warmth with which you welcomed me. A night we could never, never forget. But when morning came, what a position I was in. On the one hand your engagement to Davigan, on the other my commitment as ship's surgeon. I had signed ship's articles, I must report to the *Tasman* or be posted as a deserter. I simply had to go. The least hurtful way was to slip out without disturbing you. I thought of you continually during my enforced absence. But when I got back . . . you were married to Davigan."

Incredulity had almost supplanted the bitterness in her expression. She gave me a short laugh.

"My God, Carroll, I wouldn't have believed it possible! That you could hand me that line. You're more of a twister than ever. I'll swear you even succeed in deceiving yourself. Yes, I married Davigan."

"Then why blame me? He made you a good Catholic husband."

"You've said it, Carroll. He was the best Catholic husband the Pope ever invented."

"Meaning what?"

She took a cigarette from the pack in the pocket of her blouse and lit it.

"Since we're letting our hair down let's not spare our blushes. You've got to hear it sooner or later." She drew on her cigarette, eyes looking back in time. "You know what I'm like, how I'm made. At least you ought to."

"Yes, indeed I'll never forget how exciting . . ."

"Cut it, Carroll. You gave me the first taste of honey. And it was the last. Daniel Davigan! That man! Well, because he'd been part of the town joke for the sixteen births in his own family he was compelled by a single monstrous obsession . . . to prevent me becoming pregnant. Not by means that would help me or meet my needs, but within the permitted canon law."

"But, surely, there was little Dan."

"The fact that he came early made everything worse. Nothing ever took place at the natural times when you wanted it. Only at the mid term when I was flat out. Timing it by the calendar! Have you counted the days? I wonder if it's safe? Then the quick get rid of it, followed immediately by the "get up and make your water, squeeze hard, that's not a douche, it's permitted and it'll help." God, what a sacrifice of all fundamental decencies and dignity, and the wants of a woman's unsatisfied nature. Love according to the Catechism! Am I shocking your delicate feelings, Carroll, you're such a sweet man? Then for days after, the waiting and pestering, "Have you not come on yet?" And his sickening look of relief when I had. No expression could be lower, more hideously hypocritical than that which greeted me when I was out of action. Actually he always knew, for the deprivation I suffered intensified the distress of my periods, especially as I was forced at such times to listen to the Reverend Francis in the pulpit extolling the sacred bonds of matrimony. Even when I went to him in Confession all I got was some soulful advice at no cost to himself—prayer,

113

proper feelings, and submission to the will of God. When I pointed out that desire cannot be summoned up by the calendar I didn't get an ounce of sympathy."

These revelations, delivered with no sense of propriety, would have made tasty hearing as a demonstration of the farce of unsatisfactory conjugal performances had they not been so shamelessly bitter or so relevant to my present situation. Any temptation to laugh was stifled by my need to placate. I also already had in distant view the future possibilities in this dammed-up flood of desire. And when, after a decent pause, I thought fit to make a murmur of medical sympathy, suggesting that her tribulations were over and could be redressed, she fixed me with a look that would have chilled a polar bear.

"None of that, Doctor. After what I've been through I'm a different woman. The very mention of sex sickens me now."

"Well," I sighed, "you must blame Davigan for that, poor fellow."

"Poor fellow! A low, sickly, priest-ridden coward. I came to regard him with as much disgust as the sediment in his own chamber pot."

This was plain speaking. I felt myself justified in exploiting the situation.

"It must," I said tactfully, "have been a relief to find yourself free."

"A God-given relief." She turned and faced me. "I bless that gust of wind that blew him over."

Blew him over, what *was* this? I had to know more. I said, thoughtfully:

"Thinking it might distress you . . . I've been reluctant to press you as to how . . . ?"

"He fell off the top of the new tenement . . . just when they were finishing the upper story. He was proud of it in a stupid sort of way, the tallest block of flats in Levenford with a view, God help it, of Ben Lomond. He'd had to do with the erecting of it and of course it was on land the Davigans once owned. So that Sunday afternoon he took the boy and me up to show us. I didn't want to go, it was so windy, but he insisted, was out cat-walking on the parapet, gassing away, when . . ." She shrugged indifferently.

So that was it. I felt like saying: a sort of Ibsenish ending, the Levenford Master Builder, but this was no moment to be smart.

"He was killed?" I spoke with becoming seriousness.

"On the spot."

"Well, he's gone beyond recriminations. What good did they ever do? For that matter, if I've offended you in any way . . ." I paused significantly.

"Why don't I let you off too? No, no, Carroll. I have no malice toward you. Nevertheless . . ."

"Yes?"

"I have a use for you."

My imagination jumped ahead of me. I smiled engagingly, with just a touch of disbelief.

"After what you just said? You're kidding."

"Far from it." She glanced at me in a manner that augured ill for my future. "If you want to keep your soft, cushy, useless, no-job here, to hold on to it by the skin of your teeth, you'll have to go along with me."

What was she after? Obviously she hated me and wanted her own back. But what else? She went on:

"I'm just as sick of Levenford as you ever were, Carroll. The only offer I got there was to keep house for old Dr. Ennis when his wife died last month. Cook, clean, scrub out the surgery. And he's so far gone on the bottle now he's hardly ever sober. No, no, I don't want to go back to that stinking, scandal-ridden hole, not ever. I like it here, I like it a lot, it's heaven after what I've been through. The Matron has taken to me and she's so short of help she needs me. To cut it short, I see a chance that I never expected, to remake my life. And you're going to help me to it."

Suddenly it struck me. Could it be that after all these years she finally wanted to snaffle me. If so what a hope.

"That's impossible. They won't have a married doctor here. It's in the charter."

She gave me a lethal stare.

"Don't flatter yourself, Romeo. I'd sooner go to bed with a rattlesnake than you. All I need from you is your unwilling cooperation, a kind word to the committee, acceptance of the fact that I'm here for good. Otherwise," she paused, "you're out on your ear."

I glared at her.

"You're crazy. I like it here too and I'm going to stay. You'll never get me out of the Maybelle."

She looked me dead in the eye.

"I knew there must be something fishy about your appointment, which is more than you were ever worth.

And there is. Matron has copies of your testimonials. I've seen them and they're . . ."

"That's enough!"

"Yes, it would be a nasty word, wouldn't it? False pretenses. Might even be forgery. And what a bother it might get you into with the General Medical Council." While I listened with growing, deep-seated uneasiness, she went on. "Doctors have been struck off for less. I hope that won't be necessary. For you'd need your miserable little medical degree if I sent you back to general practice in Levenford. That's where you belong and that's where you will go if you don't toe the line. You're the one that'll go back to old Dr. Ennis. He's losing his assistant and he'd take you, on my recommendation." She gave me a thin, bitter smile. "I'm going to get a lot of pleasure watching you sweat it out here with that hanging over you."

nine

I BARGED DOWN THE HILL in a state of mind in which
rage, resentment and apprehension prevailed over the
suspicion that I was dealing with an unbalanced character. Naturally I had left her without a word. I had
found it unprofitable at any time to argue with a
woman; still less so now with one thrown off the beam
by a prolonged stretch of marital frustration. Did she
actually imagine I could be yanked out of the best,
yes, if you prefer her word, the softest crib I had ever
hoped to drop into? I was established at the Maybelle,
I now spoke German fluently—there was no need to
fake it—and on the two occasions when the committee
had visited the clinic they had expressed themselves
as fully satisfied with their choice. If the validity of
the testimonials was questioned I could explain that
I had lost the originals. And hadn't I been foreseeing
enough to protect myself against just such a contin-
gency, this threat to my security? The bold Caterina
hadn't thought of that one. I was safe. No need to

worry, Carroll, my boy. And yet I was worried. There remained with me a sense of something in the background, unspoken, unrevealed, retained, so to speak, for the *Meisterstück*. Curse that German, I meant the *coup de grace*. No, that was nonsense, yes, rot in any language. Get me back to Levenford? That noxious hole in Clydeside mud? Back to another G.P. assistantship, stuffed with night calls and surgery grinds, with an old boozer as principal, who was more or less tight half the time. She was right—it would be hell. But, never. No, not on your bleeding life, Carroll. I would fight it to the last ditch.

Suddenly, as I approached the clinic, I heard someone calling me, the voice immediately recognizable as Matron's. Perched on the rear balcony like a molting hen, she was flapping me in with a towel. Refusing to be hurried, I slowed to a walk, so that she had ample time to come down to the terrace to meet me.

"Ver haf you been, Herr Doktor?" She was practically foaming at the mouth. "*Eine Stunde* almost I am seeking you."

I permitted myself the liberty of a really dirty look, the first I had ever directed toward her.

"Where the devil do you think I've been? I'm surely entitled to a little time off. I've been taking my exercise."

I perceived with satisfaction that she was taken aback. In a modified tone, though still complaining, she declared:

"Your patient is not so good. Much sickness. All his good *Mittagessen* thrown back."

"What! Sick again?"

"Much."

"You did stop his codliver oil?"

She reddened uncomfortably.

"But it is so goot for him . . ."

"Damn it all, I told you, instructed you, to stop it."

She was silent, giving me best.

"Very well," I said shortly. "I'll have a look at him."

"*Jetzt?* Immediately?"

"When I've had a wash. He won't harm just because he's had a vomit."

This was merely to keep Hulda in her place. When she was out of sight I went across to the guest chalet.

He was lying fully dressed, on his bed, with his eyes on the ceiling. Beside him an enamel basin seemed to contain most of his lunch, but it gave out no stink of fish oil. One hand was placed protectively on his stomach. He removed it quickly as I came in, an action I did not fail to observe.

"So you've been at it again, you little rat?"

As may be imagined my mood was not attuned to sympathy and loving-kindness.

"Sorry," he said.

"You may well be. Damned little nuisance. You knew I'd put you off the oil."

"Of course. And I didn't take it. When Matron wasn't looking I poured it down the washbasin."

"You did?" This shook my preconceived opinion. "Come on then, pull up your shirt and let's have a look at you."

"It's all better now, Dr. Laurence." He half smiled. "Let's let sleeping dogs lie."

"None of that smart guff, strip to the waist."

I didn't altogether like the look of him and while he got ready I reassembled the evidence. His von Pirquet had proved negative, his temperature varied no more than a fraction of a point and beyond that cervical swelling I had found nothing specific to confirm the presence of TB or, indeed, to account for his obvious pallor, shortness of breath, palpitation and general asthenia. I began to suspect that the good Dr. Moore before leaving for the wide-open spaces had landed me with a stoumer of a diagnosis. With this in mind I took a new look, considering that recurrent sickness, giving particular attention to the abdomen. As I had previously observed, his was somewhat distended, but this "big belly" was a not uncommon feature in the rundown children who came to the Maybelle, and I had rather taken it for granted. Now, however, I began carefully to palpate. Once again everything seemed in order, but suddenly there it was: I no more than caught the edge of it: a tender and slightly swollen spleen.

"That hurts you?"

"Somewhat . . . yes, a little," he admitted, wincing despite the understatement.

"Does it pain you when I don't press? I mean when you're up and around."

"Not really . . . just a sort of dragging feeling sometimes."

So now what? A palpable, tender spleen, at that age,

and instinctively my eyes went back to the inner surface of his arms on which I could just make out a faint
purpuric staining of the skin. It had me puzzled.

"Nothing bad I hope, Dr. Laurence?"

My silence had worried him.

"Don't be a toad. This probably means you don't
have TB at all. Coming here with a false tag on you
and all that rot about scrofula."

He looked at me doubtfully.

"That's a relief. Or isn't it?"

I ignored this and said: "What else have you been
hiding, you little coward? You've had these sick attacks
for some time?"

"For a little while. But when they pass off I'm quite
hungry and can eat anything."

"What about these red blotches on your skin?"

"Well, yes, I've had them off and on. But they fade
very quickly. I thought they might be just an irrita-
tion."

"Naturally." Then I took a shot in the dark. "Have
you had bleeding recently from the inside of your
mouth, I mean from your gums?"

His eyes widened with surprise and, actually, ad-
miration.

"That's remarkably clever of you, Dr. Laurence.
Yes, as a matter of fact I have. But I think, I mean, I
thought it was my hard toothbrush."

I was silent, staring at him with ill-concealed mis-
giving intensified by this sudden and unanticipated
prospect of further trouble. What had I let myself in
for? Wasn't it enough to be saddled with his bitch of

123

a mother? There wasn't a trace of TB in this obnoxious little smartie. At a guess I was faced by one of these obscure idiopathic blood syndromes, of which there were probably a score of different varieties, conditions that never properly clear up, run on for years, and break the back of the average G.P. with the need for repeated tests, to say nothing of probable hemorrhages and transfusions. I would not stand for it. In this instance my own modification of the Hippocratic oath was never more applicable: when stuck with a difficult and prolonged case, get rid of it. Yes, I would put through a couple of basic tests and if the results spelled trouble he would have to go to the hospital. The Winton Victoria would take him if he proved pathologically interesting. With a brightening of my mood, I reflected that if he were sent home his mother could have no excuse for remaining at the clinic. I would be rid of them both, kill two birds with one stone, and be free again.

Naturally I could not fling any of this at him. He had been watching me intently as if trying to discover what was going on in my head. Assuming an air of cheerful camaraderie, a useful aspect of my best bedside manner, I picked up the enamel basin.

"Can't have you wasting good food like this, young fellow. We'll have to do something about it."

"You can?"

"Why not? There's nothing wrong with your stomach. You're anemic. I'll just take a sample of your blood to make sure."

"Bleed me? Like the old apothecaries?"

"Oh, cut out that nonsense! This is simple, and scientific. It won't hurt you a bit."

I had some difficulty in finding and puncturing his saphenous vein, which was almost threadlike, but he was quite good about it, almost too passive. I drew off five cc's, stoppered the test tube after I had smeared several slides, exclaimed cheerfully:

"There we are. When these slides are dry we'll stain them. By tomorrow we'll know all about your red corpuscles. You can even take a peep at them under the microscope yourself."

That perked him up slightly.

"What an interesting situation. A boy examining his own blood. What about that little tube?"

"We'll use that for your blood hemoglobin, and," I added indefinitely, "other things." He was obviously admiring me a lot and I scarcely liked to admit I would send it to the Kantonspital in Zurich. "Now relax for a bit. I must let them know in the kitchen about your diet."

"Bread and water?" He gave me a wan smile.

"You deserve it. Still, what would you like?"

"I'm rather hungry now after that emptying." He thought for a moment. "Mashed potatoes and," with another smile, "the meence."

Impossible not to smile back at him.

"We'll consider it. At least you can have the mash and some of that good gravy. Now cheer up. I'll do what I can for you."

I went out of the room with my own words ringing derisively in my ears. "I'll do what I can for you." Well, damn it, I would—at least I'd do as much as I reasonably could.

Naturally I avoided the office where I knew that both of my enemies would be expecting me. Instead I lit a cigarette and went into the test room. It wouldn't hurt the kid to wait for his supper, and although I had told him I would leave the slides till the morning—since I did not want him cliff-hanging on my neck all evening—I was rather curious to have a look at them.

Still smoking, I stained them, a quick simple job, and put one on the stage of the excellent Leitz. Rather than waste my cigarette, one of the oval Abdullas Lotte got me duty free through her airline, I sat down comfortably and finished it before rising to take a look.

At first I thought my oil immersion lens was maladjusted, but as I focused and refocused the same picture came up. It made me catch my breath. Although I am no virtuoso as a biologist there was no mistaking this—it hit me full in the eye. Fascinating, actually, in its own morbid manner, the sort of thing you might never see once in a G.P.'s lifetime. This was it: the field crammed with lymphocytes, white corpuscles multiplied five or six times over. I could even make out immature forms, myelocytes, large immature corpuscles from the bone marrow never present in healthy blood. Obvious, of course, what was taking place. A hyperplasia of white cell precursors in the bone marrow, progressive and uncontrolled, crowding out the progenitors of red cells and platelets, probably even eroding the bone itself. I clipped on the second slide with the measuring scale, dropped on fresh oil, and made a rough count on one square and multiplied. That settled it.

I could scarcely unlatch myself from the eyepiece. It was one of those moments, so rare in my dreary run of the mill experience, when you strike the exceptional, have been good enough to uncover it, then see the whole sequence of events, past, present and future, laid before you. The future? I had to stop patting myself on the back. This was bad news for young Capablanca—in fact the worst. Oddly enough, at the airport, the first time I sighted his sad little pan, I felt he was unlucky, marked out in some queer way for disaster. Born for trouble, out of that impossible failure of a marriage, the mark of the Davigans upon him. And now he'd had it. Still, though God knew it was the last thing I would have wanted, there was no denying that it solved my problem. I thought this over thoroughly for several minutes, then took up both slides and went into the office.

They were both waiting for me, one on either side of my desk, the brave Hulda actually occupying my chair. She looked at me uncomfortably, but with a glint of defiance, which told me they had been putting in more overtime on my character.

"Ve attend to ask what is for Daniel's supper."

"Later." I brushed it aside. "If I can have my desk, Matron?"

I stood there waiting for her to get up, which she did, though with reluctance. When I had seated myself

I faced up to the widow Davigan. That was how I meant to think of her now, or simply as Davigan, she had joined the tribe of her own free will, and after all she never called me anything but Carroll, and I would let her have it straight. She could expect no mercy from this throne.

"It's like this," I said. "For some time I've suspected that we've been misled by a false diagnosis. We're not dealing with a tubercular infection. Your boy has never had TB."

"Then what . . . ?" She broke off suspiciously.

"I've just made a blood smear. Here are the slides. They show a massive increase in the white cells. Instead of the normal five to ten thousand lymphocytes per cubic millimeter there's not far short of sixty thousand . . . plus an abnormal proliferation of myelocytes."

This meant nothing to her, but it chilled the Matron.

"You are not serious, Herr Doktor?"

I liked that Herr Doktor, the first in several days.

"Only too serious, unfortunately."

Davigan was looking confusedly from me to the Matron.

"This is something bad?"

"It coot be . . . but *natürlich* we are not sure."

I cut in firmly.

"I regret having to tell you that I'm only too sure. It's an open and shut case. The boy has myelocytic leukocythemia."

Did Davigan really get the message of these two words? I think not. At least, not entirely, for she didn't wilt. She flushed up and her suspicions of me, never absent, deepened.

"I don't understand this sudden change and I don't like it."

"Are you suggesting that I like it, or that I'm in any way responsible for the sudden change?"

"It's all very peculiar . . . I don't understand . . ."

"We have been trying to make you understand."

The Matron, recovering herself, suddenly cut in.

"Who is ve? Caterina *hat recht*. There must come more advice. *Ein zweiter* opinion, *und der beste.* You must bring specialist Herr Professor Lamotte from Zurich."

"You'd only be wasting his time. And he has none to waste. Anyhow, he'd never come this far . . ."

"Then you must take the boy to him at the Kantonspital," Hulda persisted.

On the point of refusing, I suddenly changed my mind. A second opinion, particularly Lamotte's, would take the pressure off me. They could never get around his diagnosis. It must stick. And that was all I needed. I was calm, quite sure of myself.

"Very well. I agree. I'll ring up and make an appointment for the earliest possible day. Meantime," I turned to Matron, "as you were so anxious about Daniel's supper, perhaps you'll see that he gets some *consommé* and *kartoffel purée* with meat gravy."

She had something to say, but thought better of it. When she had gone I stood up, and made for the door. But Cathy caught me on the way out. Her flush had left her. She looked drawn, tight-lipped.

"I know you're up to something, Carroll, so I'm warning you. Don't try any of your dirty tricks on me or it'll be the worse for you."

I stared her out, in chilly silence. What else could you do with such a troll?

ten

THE ZÜRICH KANTONSPITAL is agreeably situated on the
Zürichberg, in a residential district high up on the
left bank of the Limmat. An excellent site typically
ill chosen, since approaching from the river by the
interminable line of steep steps, you are halfway
to a coronary by the time you get there. The hospital is a massive structure, lamentably in the Swiss
taste, with modern additions, offset by some tall and
beautiful old trees, and to such patients as may be
interested, it affords a striking view of three ancient
churches; the Predigerkirche, the Grossmünster and
the Fraumünster which, with the innumerable banks,
suggest the split personality of this city—a devotion
to both Mammon and the Lord.

On Saturday afternoon, of the following week, I
came through the swinging doors and out of the Medical Department with Daniel. It was a beautiful day
and as the late autumn sunshine and crisp cool air
greeted us he let out a long breath of relief.

"Well, Dr. Laurence, I'm glad that's over."

He gave a bit of a laugh and took my hand, an action which, I need not add, embarrassed me acutely, gave me what in Scotland is called the grue. I was not in the best of moods. After all my trouble in making the appointment I had been hung up for most of the afternoon with only two quick chances to telephone Lotte, trying to explain why I was in Zurich without seeing her, and getting pretty well told off for my pains. Still, in the circumstances, I could not do other than let him drag on to me.

"Surely it wasn't too bad?" I said.

"Oh, no. I liked Dr. Lamotte. Very serious, with that way he has of reading right through you. But he gave me such a nice smile as I was leaving. He's clever, isn't he?"

"He's the tops," I said shortly. "French-Swiss. They're the best . . . intellectually."

"But I never thought he would send me in to all those young ladies, doing all sorts of things to me."

"Those girls are technicians . . . each trained to do a special test."

"Such as?"

"Well, more or less everything, for example, find out all about your corpuscles, and of course your blood group."

"But couldn't you have done that, Dr. Laurence?"

"Naturally, if I had their equipment. You're a group AB if you want to know."

"Is that quite regular?"

"Perfectly. It's the rarest of all the blood groups."

"What group are you?"

"I'm group O."

"They did seem rather interested in my blood." He reflected. "Perhaps it isn't blue enough." He looked up as if expecting me to smile. "I hope Dr. Lamotte gave you a good account of me."

"Of course he did," I said, freeing myself from his sweaty little clutch to give him a reassuring pat on the back. "We'll have a chat about it presently."

We walked through the avenue of plane trees, the dry fallen leaves crackling under our feet. I'd had nothing but a cold beef sandwich for lunch so I said:

"We'll have something to eat before we start back."

"Good!" he said cheerfully. "As a matter of fact, now it's all over, I'm quite peckish, and ready for anything."

This silenced me for the moment.

We got into the Opel station wagon, which I had parked in the hospital lot, and I took him to Sprungli's, which at this hour between lunch and five o'clock was not overcrowded. Upstairs at a window table I ordered poached eggs on toast, hot milk for him, café crème for myself.

"None of these lovely cakes?" he hinted. "Remember, we had a sort of agreement . . ."

"You'll have a couple after your eggs." What the hell did it matter anyway. Let him have some fun while it lasted.

As I watched his pale-skinned, tight face brighten, I looked quickly out of the window, barely seeing the heavy traffic moving in the Bahnhofstrasse or the long

133

low blue trams swinging round the island with the newspaper kiosk in the Parade Platz.

Classic leukocythemia. Malignant myelocytic type: cause still unknown. Lamotte had flattered me by confirming my diagnosis, putting a few knobs on by way of ornament. Relentlessly progressive. The multiplying abnormal cells colonizing the various organs of the body—choking liver, spleen, kidneys, lungs, proliferating in the bone marrow, pouring out more and more from the bone marrow. Symptoms: acute weakness and wasting, big belly, hemorrhage from the stomach and bowels, edema of the feet and legs from obstruction of the lymphatic vessels. Treatment: specific medication unknown; radiations in small doses inadequate, larger doses destroy the few healthy cells; in emergencies, blood transfusions. Prognosis: indeterminate yet inevitably fatal. Minimum, six months, at the most, three years.

Too bad, naturally. But he was not the first kid to get his marching orders. I had a sudden recollection of the epidemic of cerebrospinal meningitis I had come up against in the Rhondda. How many dirty blankets had I pulled over those poor little stiffs? No wonder you get tough. Quickly, I shook it off, and took a slug of coffee. The groundwork had to be laid and better now than later. When he was well into his second egg I leaned forward.

"How is the grub?"

"First rate."

"Good. That's part of your treatment—no more cod-

liver oil but lots of protein. I think I did mention that
you are anemic."

"Oh, you did. You were the one who really spotted it.
Did . . . did Dr. Lamotte agree?"

I nodded.

"And your treatment's all worked out for you." I
paused, then added cheerfully: "It's just a pity that we
can't work on the important part of it at the Maybelle."

His mouth opened like a hooked trout's, and a piece
of egg dropped off his fork.

"Why not?"

"We haven't got the facilities."

He digested that slowly.

"Couldn't I go to the Kantonspital? Like today?"

"I'm afraid not, Daniel. It's too far from Schlewald.
You need regular treatment. And the natural place for
you to get it is the Victoria Hospital at home."

His chin really dropped, down into his thin chicken's
neck.

"You mean, go back to Levenford?"

"Why not, boy?" I laughed. "You live there, don't
you?"

"Yes," he said slowly. "I did live there. But I . . .
Mother said . . . we were hoping we might spend a
longer time in Switzerland."

"I was hoping so too, but needs must . . . and what's
wrong with dear old Levenford?"

He was silent, his eyes on his plate.

I've not been particularly happy there since my
father died."

"You miss him?"

"I suppose I do. But it's not . . . not quite that."

"What then?"

He had gone white round the lips and suddenly I wanted to rise, get the bill, and clear out to the car. But something held me there, bending toward him, waiting for the answer. And it came. Speaking slowly, not looking at me, he said:

"When my father died, or was killed falling off the roof, there was a lot of unpleasant talk." He paused, and the thought hit me like an electric shock: no wonder Mama doesn't want to go back to Levenford.

"Yes, Danny?" I prompted.

"Boys shouted things after me. And at the inquest, after Canon Dingwall told me . . ."

He broke off, raising his head pitifully to look at me, and I saw the tears running down his cheeks. How low can you get, Carroll? Cut it out, for God's sake. You've heard more than enough.

"Come, Danny boy. Not a word more. You know we wouldn't upset you for the world. Here, take my handkerchief and I'll pop over to the counter for your cakes."

In five minutes, playing it good and hearty, I had him dried off and polished up, eating a meringue with no more than an occasional sniffle.

On the way to the car, which I had parked in Tielstrasse, I hoped it wouldn't happen, but it did. First the hand, then the usual:

"Thank you for being so decent to me, Dr. Laurence."

But when you are Carroll you can brush off compunction after no more than a brief, bad moment. Self-preservation is the first law of nature. Anything by the name of Davigan had always spelled poison for me, I positively had to get rid of them. I had nothing against this little semi-animated bit of gray matter, but the mother would kill me. Always she would have her knife in me and one day, so help me, she would out me from the Maybelle.

As we got into the car the sky had turned to a livid gray and a few soft flakes came fluttering down.

"You see, Daniel," I reasoned. "It's beginning to snow. Soon we'll be into winter and that's not very suitable for you."

"I like snow," he said, and looking up at the lovely feathery drift he muttered, half to himself as if explaining it away: "It's just the angels having a pillow fight."

"They must be knocking the hell out of themselves," I said—it was getting thicker. I left it at that, revved the engine and set off.

It was not an easy drive, the deicer wasn't working too well and at one point, near Coire, I thought I might have to stop and fit chains. But at the back of ten o'clock we reached the Maybelle.

I dropped the boy at the chalet where his mother was waiting to put him to bed, and went on to the main building. Matron, alerted by the headlights of the car—for the snow muffled all sound—was at the door to meet me, and her manner, while restrained and formal was, to my surprise, not hostile.

"*Schlechte Nacht*, Herr Doktor. You have managed

vell to come safely." Then, as I shed my coat and scarf: "*Haben Sie Hunger?*"

"I've had practically nothing to eat all day."

She nodded and turned away. Further surprises lay ahead. In my room the stove had been freshly stoked, the table was set for supper, and almost at once the old battle-ax came in with a tray on which I made out a tureen of steaming soup and something I had not seen in years—a big ashet holding the good remaining half of a steak and kidney pie.

I couldn't wait to get into it but, softened, not sitting down, I said:

"I suppose you want to hear everything."

"*Nein*, Herr Doktor." As I stared at her she went on: "You must forgive. Caterina becomes so anxious and I alzo, that I did telephone the ward sister of Dr. Lamotte. Ve know all, alas. Alzo that everything you have said of this bad illness is absolute and correct."

This from Hulda was a very handsome amende—if I hadn't been so chilled I might have glowed. But as I eased into my chair and began to ladle out the soup, she went on:

"Zo now, vithout question it is settled that Caterina and the boy must remain. This afternoon I wrote express to Herr Scrygemour telling how undispensable she becomes to me, so long without proper assistance. He will consent. It is sure. And so, Herr Doktor I wish you *gute Nacht.*"

With that she bobbed me that recently developed formal little bow and went out.

After the soup I ate the steak and kidney pie, slowly,

and thoughtfully, savoring the flavor of good Scottish food. I ate all of it, and it couldn't have been tastier. The brave Caterina had certainly been putting in more good work on Hulda, than whom no one liked better to feed well. So be it, let them have it their way for the present. I held the card that was the clincher. At the moment it was not up my sleeve, but it would be, for I knew where to find it.

After I had finished, though I was full to the ears and all in with tiredness, I sat down determinedly and wrote the Circulation Department of the Levenford *Herald* requesting their report on the Davigan inquest by return of post.

eleven

I HAD A FOUL NIGHT. So far I have refrained from elaborating on the extraordinary fantasy that afflicts me. It is a personal matter. It worries me. And as it is patently a hallucination, both auditory and visual, I prefer to keep it to myself. Nevertheless, lately the attacks have been more frequent and last night I suffered one of unprecedented severity. In fact, a shattering nightmare.

It began as usual. Darkness and desolation in the strange silent city. A sense of heartbreaking loneliness and the need, immediate and terrible, to seek help, to escape. Then, after that moment of fearful anticipation, the slow footsteps beginning, following, deliberate and insistent, echoing from behind me in the empty street.

I began to run. Usually I ran with speed. But tonight my feet were weighted and by the greatest effort I achieved only a dragging trot. The sounds behind me increased, drew gradually nearer. I must be overtaken. Almost, I could feel the touch of that unseen hand upon my shoulder. I swerved into an alley. Immediately I was in a network of narrow streets lined with low windows, each curtained red, and open, offering some hope of refuge and escape. But as, one by one, I stretched toward them a wind arose and blew in gusts along the narrow alleys, slamming the windows shut. Now I had reached an empty square, enclosed by tall half-ruined buildings, through which I toiled in a breathless sweat, and still relentlessly pursued.

The syndrome was lasting longer, much longer than before, the more so since this final enclosure appeared to offer no possible exit. To be trapped so abjectly was more than I could bear. I would not endure it and at last, flinging myself into the doorway of a deserted warehouse, I forced myself to face about and at the pitch of my lungs to shout toward that invisible approach.

"Keep away. Don't come near me!"

Instantly I heard the signal of release, the low, distant baying of a hound, and in the same second the rush of footsteps ceased. The pursuit was over, once again, though by the skin of my teeth, I had escaped.

In the morning when I half awoke with a ringing head, it took an effort to pull myself together. Yet it was some relief to realize that it was Sunday and I could drowse on until ten o'clock. When the holiday groups were here Sunday could be a trial but lately it had treated me handsomely since Matron, who regularly attended the eight o'clock Mass, had taken both the Davigans with her. So although I always set out, book in hand, before eleven-thirty to keep in good standing with Hulda, I rarely lingered near the church but, by a convenient detour, reached the station kiosk for a chat with Gina or, more profitably, the Pfeffermühle where they kept an admirable light beer.

I got up at half past ten and after breakfast which, although served without *ballons,* I did not want, I hoofed through the usual routine ward visit, where I decided to mark one of the boys for an early discharge. His pleurisy had cleared up nicely and his parents had written, wanting him home. Then, before taking off for the town, I crossed to the chalet to have a quick look at young Davigan. He met me, fully dressed, at the door.

"They let me sleep in, Dr. Laurence. So I'm going with you this morning."

This was an unexpected snag. Critically, I looked him over—he was smiling, seemed better and well rested after the soneryl I had given him. It was not altogether unexpected. I saw that he was on the uplift, surely one of the most pitiful manifestations of the myelocytic brand of leukemia, a sudden inexplicable improvement which arouses false hopes only to be followed invariably by a relapse.

"You're an invalid," I said. "You're not obliged to . . . to come to church."

"Oh, I wouldn't miss it for anything. Especially with you."

Could anything be more sickening than this unwanted and too open devotion? This morning especially. If he had not been so ill I would have given him a flat "no." Instead, I tried to think up an excuse. No luck. Nothing else for it then, I was stuck with him, otherwise there would be a shindy. I had a feeling in the small of my back that eyes were watching from windows.

"Let's go then," I said, with false optimism, putting my hands carefully in my pockets to avoid the clutch.

It was the kind of morning that follows a snowfall in the Grisons—a sky blue as a mandril's behind, a sparkling sun making false diamonds of the snow crystals and a crisp air that tingled and made you want to lose your headache and live forever. In Switzerland they know how to deal with snow, and the village council, well disposed toward the Maybelle, had swept and banked our drive all the way down to the main well-scoured highway. We walked between walls of a dazzling blue whiteness that stung the eyes, mine, at least. The village roofs were heavily blanketed and as we moved along the bells began, the waves of sound showering us with icy particles from the projecting eaves.

"An avalanche." The encumbrance laughed. "Let's pretend we're crossing the Alps. Three cheers for Hannibal and us."

We went into the church. After the exterior brightness it seemed darker, gloomier than ever, the congregation scanty and scattered—on a day like this most people came to the earlier service. He had made, of course, for the front row.

I have already reported my allergy to churches. They give me a low feeling, a sinking nostalgia, plus an angry "let's get the hell out of it" sensation, in all, a complex especially aggravated by this particular church. Outside it was fantastic, inside so like a tomb it struck me with the chill of the anatomy room where I had dissected my first cadaver, and on the reredos, a raw red granite wall, there was a great flat carving, a sort of impressionist bas relief in the same red granite that always got me down. It was the Man, of course, not on the Cross, nothing conventional or agonized, just the profile and an outline, the suggestion of a figure, bent forward, and half turned toward you, with one arm stretched forward. It killed me, that figure. Your eyes kept going back to it, not only because it was a damn fine original piece of work, totally at variance with the tiddy design of the church, but because if you didn't disconnect the contact and tell yourself, as I did: Forget it, you were liable to start going back over things best forgotten.

I had scarcely knelt down and gone through the usual sketchy motions, to save my face, when the local father appeared, not yet robed. He was a thin little man who looked ill, a Pole with a name like Zobronski, if that is how he spelled it—Swiss clergy were scarce in this remote end of the valley, they had to make do with political refugees. He was conning the congregation with an upturned forefinger.

"He wants a server?" The words were hissed in my ear. "I'll go."

And before I could grip him he was up and away. The moment I came in I'd had a premonition that things would go ill for me. When he reappeared, in a natty red cassock and white surplice, looking like the boy Pope, and began to light the candles with an expertise he could only have acquired from Dingwall, I began to sweat down the back of my neck. It was worse when the Mass began. You never saw such a showoff. This little upstart knew all the tricks. I kept hoping he would trip on the hassock or drop the book, but he never put a hand or a foot wrong, and all with such an air of presanctified devotion he might have been performing before a bevy of Cardinals in the Sistine Chapel. Zobronski, if that was his name, seemed to go along with the act. Other times he had been a fairly scrubby performer and you kept noticing how much he coughed, or that he'd cut himself shaving, or that the cuffs of his pants were frayed and his boots practically worn out. Now, however, you would have thought he had money in the bank, he was putting a few flourishes in on his own.

When it came to the Communion I bet myself the little pain in the neck wouldn't take it, he had been too long away from Confession. But he did, and the way he shut his eyes turned me over. Most of the congregation went up and as he passed up and down the rails with the paten I felt the corner of one of his eyes slanted toward me. What a hope! How long was it now since they caught me? Must be more than five years, since that Mission at Nottingham. I went in for a lark, to hear that Franciscan, Father Aloysius—they said he was dramatic, as good as Charles Laughton— and came out reconverted. I had kept it up, too, for a couple of months until I met that redhead North of Ireland nurse from the local hospital. She was a dandy too, except for that Belfast accent. For a bet she could crack glasses with it in the Sherwood Bar.

After the blessing I went out to the clean fresh air and waited for him. He did not keep me long, and came out spry and cheerful. I did not respond.

"The father was so anxious to meet you, Dr. Laurence. D'you know he speaks four languages?"

"Don't mix me up with that Pole. He needs money."

"Oh, yes, he's terribly poor. A big debt was made building the church. And now he's running things on practically nothing. That's why there's so little oil for heating. I don't think he even gets enough to eat."

"That's his problem," I said. "Mine is to get the *Sunday Times*. We're going to the station."

As we set off he said:

"Did you see that wonderful carving on the wall?"

"Only when I looked at it, which is something I avoid."

"Apparently it was done by a young sculptor who was ill in Davos."

"Then he died." I shot it at him. "The masterpiece was his last act."

"Oh, no. He got cured and is quite famous now. He has an exhibition in Vienna this year."

"Let's go," I said. "I can't wait. Now come on and don't be so full of yourself."

You couldn't shake him. He had about him a kind of glow. Was it due to these few extra red corpuscles he had managed to manufacture overnight? I doubted it.

We were at the kiosk and the Sunday papers were in, which gave me a slight lift. It made a dull day for me when they missed the connection at Zurich. I bought my *Times*, without much palaver, and was turning away when he said:

"Could you change me a half crown into Swiss money, Dr. Laurence?"

"You have a half crown?"

"Naturally." He smiled. "The old Canon gave it me before I left. And now we have snow I'd very much like to send him one of these pictures." He pointed to a color postcard of a big St. Bernard and a pup, both with brandy flasks around their necks.

"I'll give you fifty centimes for the card," I said, thinking how often this old bag of bones came up between us. "You can bore a hole in the half crown and wear it round your neck."

I regretted that immediately I had said it. But he did not seem to mind.

"It wouldn't be very spendable there. Besides, I already have a medal that he gave me."

I bought the card and lent him my ballpoint. Although I was curious, I avoided looking at what he wrote since I felt he would show me the effusion, and he did.

Dear Very Reverend Canon,

Your pupil and esteemed chess enemy sends you greetings from the Alps where in company of [scored out] with his psyician he has just passed through an avalansh, small but troublesome. These two St. Bernards, the large with brandy for Dr. Laurence, the small with lemonade for me, were

fortunately not needed. I am very well today, but
may be coming back soon. So beware of P to K4
with the Ruy Lopez opening.

"Two mistakes in spelling," was all I could say.

"Yes, I'm an awful speller," he agreed. "It's my
Achilles heel."

Yet the effort was commendably neat, so I softened
and bought him a stamp from Gina who, all through,
had watched the proceedings with particular interest.
I knew she would rib me mercilessly later.

"You're quite attached to old Dingwall?" I said, as
we walked off.

"Oh, yes . . . closely," he said seriously. "He's always
been so kind to us, lately especially."

"After the . . . the accident?"

He nodded, expansively. "You know, Dr. Laurence,
it's something for a boy of my age to be, well, trusted
by someone like Canon Dingwall."

"Who wouldn't be?" I said encouragingly. "Still . . ."
I smiled. "I don't quite see how he'd need to trust a
little nipper like you."

"But he does."

"In what way?" I laughed.

"To keep a secret." This came out proudly, then his
face closed down as though he had said too much.

"I can't believe it."

"But it's true," he persisted.

"Then won't you let me into it?"

He kept silent, still with that shut expression, then
he looked up at me.

"I couldn't," he said slowly, "although I would like to very much. You see . . . you can't break the seal of confession."

This was one out of the bag that I would never have dreamed of. But I couldn't push it too far. I had to drop it for the time being. I must wait for that report from the Levenford *Herald*. But I was not at all discouraged. Something queer, decidedly queer and more than decidedly suspicious, lay beneath all this, well below the surface, deep down in fact, but sooner or later if I kept digging I would strike pay dirt. These, I reflected, not without satisfaction, might prove to be appropriate words.

We had reached the end of the platform before he spoke again.

"I hope you're not offended?"

"Oh, no," I said, on just the right note of hurt reluctance. "I'd never want to come between Dingwall and you."

Nothing more was said until we were outside the station, then he made an obvious effort to change the subject.

"There's nothing else we can do, now we're in the village? I'm feeling so . . . sort of well. No chance of that game of chess?"

"They'll all be out on a day like this," I said. "But if you like we'll stop in at the Pfeffermühle for a drink."

We did just that, stepping off the side road into the snug little dark-beamed stube. As I had expected, it was empty. I gave him an apfelsaft and had an Eichberger. The place seemed to thrill him and when he saw the cups of the Chess Club, most of which had been won by Bemmel, the former schoolmaster, he made me promise to bring him back again. When he saw on the notice board the name Schach Club, he gave out that brainy little yelp, prelude to the exposition of some special tidbit of knowledge.

"Schach! How very interesting, Dr. Laurence. Don't you see, deriving directly from Shah. Of course chess too is a corruption of that word, though less obvious."

"What are you driveling about?"

"Chess was the Shah's special game and is believed to have originated in ancient Persia."

"You're kidding. It's as old as that?"

"Terribly old, and royal. A favorite of ever so many kings, like Charlemagne and Harun al-Raschid. Even King Canute played it."

"Wasn't he too busy with the waves?"

"Far from it. There's a historical record of a game he played with a courtier named Earl Ulf, which he lost and got up in a rage knocking over the board. Oddly enough, two days later Earl Ulf was mysteriously murdered."

He looked so serious I burst out laughing and, after a shocked moment, he joined me. We both laughed our heads off over the end of Ulf.

Strangely enough, my mood had mellowed, not entirely due to the good beer. Things were beginning to work well for me. And I did not mind young Davigan showing off in this sort of atmosphere, I was getting used to him, in fact I almost liked him. All the way home he talked his head off. Even when we got back after one o'clock he couldn't keep his trap shut. They were both waiting for us, Davigan and the Matron, and the soup tureen was on the table.

"You are late, Herr Doktor." Hulda made meaningful play with the watch that was always pinned on to her left protuberance.

"You must forgive us, Matron," the kid yodeled. "We've had such a nice time and we stopped for a drink at the Pfeffermühle."

You could almost see Hulda's hair rise. The widow was giving me a nasty look.

"Ach so, the Pfeffermühle. That is *kein Platz* for Sonntag. And to take the leetle boy."

"What is it?" said Davigan.

"A low drinkplace for low peoples."

All the rungs I had made on the ladder slipped away from me, I was down, with a bump.

The *Mittagessen* began and ended in silence. They had ganged up on me again. Never mind, Carroll, your time will come. And soon.

twelve

THE BRITISH POSTAL SERVICES have neither the speed nor the accuracy of the Swiss, and the response to my letter to the Levenford *Herald* did not arrive until Thursday morning of the following week. But it was more than worth the delay. The *Herald* had splashed the inquiry on the front page and beyond a full report of the proceedings had added a special article on the legal aspects of the case which I found particularly illuminating.

Naturally, I devoured that worthy paper, even letting my coffee cool, in my haste to get to the meat of the news. Then I read everything with extreme care, and with a growing interest and satisfaction. This was all I needed, had hoped for, had indeed expected. I lit up an Abdulla and took a long, deep aromatic breath. What a beautiful day! The sun shone into my little sitting room, a mavis was whistling outside my window, all was well with the world of the Hon. L. Carroll.

During the forenoon I was bright, cheerful, and in no hurry. The Davigan had been so beastly to me lately, anticipation became a greater pleasure. I chose the appropriate moment with due care and circumspection. I waited until after the *Mittagessen* when Matron, always a heavy eater, took her usual catnap in her room. The brain trust, well wrapped, was stowed away on the far, sunny side of the terrace. From my window I saw Davigan cross to the chalet. I gave her ten minutes then took a leisurely stroll over.

There had been heavy rain during the week, clearing away much of the snow, and the lower pastures were green again, sappy with verdure. The cows, turned out for a brief spell, were jangling around nosing each other skittishly and cropping the succulent grass like mad. From the rain-swollen valley below came the soothing hum of the distant waterfall. In the spring there would be trout in that deep pool. I liked it all better than before, and soon it would safely be mine again.

I tapped on the chalet door, waited. There was no answer. I stepped in and at once, as she had not heard me, I had a fair uncensored view of her.

She was in the little kitchen behind the living room, with the sleeves of her blouse rolled up, ironing some of Daniel's shirts and, if you can believe it, singing. I had never heard her sing before and she hadn't a bad voice either. Ninety-nine percent of Scottish songs are sad, filled with broken trysts, absconded lovers, drowned miller's daughters, or downright laments choked up with sentimental longings for the isles, lochs, hills and heather that make up most of that poor bleeding neglected orphan of a country. But this was one of the happy songs and she sang it happily. Yes, I could see that she was happy, fancying herself nicely dug in, and with no real idea of the boy's illness. From the first she had never believed a word I had told her, and the ever-loving Hulda had considerately kept back the worst of the bad news.

Sail bonny boat like a bird on the wing.

She paused for a minute to change the iron. In that kitchen we had no electric iron switch and she was heating them on the stove. Once it was in the shield she put out a neat little spit and saw it sizzle off. I liked that neat little spit—it was human, but it wouldn't get her off the hook. Satisfied, she resumed the ironing and the song.

Over the sea to Skye.
Carry the lad that is born to be king.

Believe it or not, although I have just panned them, I am a sucker for these old Scots ballads, perhaps it is my Bruce blood responding. They soften me up. It was time for me to go in, before I started to hum an accompaniment.

The instant I appeared she gave a slight start and stopped the song, but went on with the ironing. After a moment, not looking up, she said:

"Well, Carroll, what are you selling today? A cheap line in smutty postcards?"

"No," I said. "But I'll see what I can do for you if you're interested."

"I'm not. And I'm busy. So let's have it."

"It's nothing of importance," I said easily. "But somebody seems to have sent me this."

And I handed her the Levenford *Herald*.

Now she did stop. She put the iron on the stand and, as she saw the date, her face changed. The color drained out of it.

"Sent you?" she said. "The Davigans . . . they'll never let me be . . . but they don't know I'm here." Her brows suddenly drew together. "No, of course . . . You . . . you wrote for it."

"I will admit to a little natural curiosity," I said, shrugging it off. "I was naturally interested in my old friend's accident, and you were so reticent I thought I'd go to the fountainhead."

"The fountainhead! And your old friend! Carroll, you'll make me die laughing."

"I hope not. At least not until we've had a little chat. Now I'm no expert on Scots law, but from this worthy paper I learn that it was the Procurator Fiscal, instructed by the police, who petitioned the Sheriff to hold the Public Inquiry."

She pushed back a strand of hair from her forehead, disconcerted by this approach. I parked on a convenient chair and went on.

"The Sheriff then granted the petition, witnesses were cited at the notice of the Procurator Fiscal, and the Inquiry was held by the Sheriff and a Jury of seven, relatives of the deceased being entitled to be represented by a solicitor."

"Why are you giving me this!" she said angrily. "Don't I know it."

"Because, in the first place, the solicitor for the Davigan family did not represent you."

"Thank God, he did not."

"And in everything he said, he expressed the general feeling of doubt as to how your late husband managed to slip off that parapet. Of course you told me it was a very windy day."

I thought she would deny it but, no, she said, in a hard voice:

"Yes, I did tell you."

"But at the Inquiry, the Fiscal made it a big point that it was a completely windless day."

She was silent, then she said:

"I was unconsciously defending myself when I invented that wind for you, Carroll. I knew what was in your mind then, and what is in it now. You think I shoved Dan over."

"No." I half shook my head. "Still, the Davigans seemed to have that in mind. Dan's father came out with some rough stuff in the witness box."

"He's always had his knife in me, that old ram. And since he went bankrupt he's practically halfwitted."

"But the Fiscal," I reasoned, "even he expressed his doubts, you might even say his suspicions . . . that a man, shown by the evidence of the pathologist who did the post mortem to be in perfect health, with no evidence of heart trouble or cerebral condition that might cause collapse, a man who was, in addition, a seasoned builder, well trained to heights, should, on a dead calm day, suddenly . . ."

"I know all that, Carroll," she cut in. "I heard him say it."

"Then the piece of your dress, torn from your sleeve, still clenched in Dan's hand when they got to him."

"That was highly inconvenient for me. Naturally, it was his grab to save himself as I pushed. Almost damning, wasn't it, Carroll? But the police did not think so, or they would have prosecuted me."

"Yes, on criminal charges," I murmured. "It was fortunate you got the verdict. Though it was not unanimous. A split four to three, wasn't it?"

"It was enough. And afterwards I was congratulated by both the solicitor for the employers and the Inspector of Factories—who was officially present. They said my behavior was above reproach."

I had to admire her, controlling her nerves under that deadpan calm. She was tough. But no more than me.

"I'm well aware of your saintly disposition. And of course, by the split verdict you were technically exonerated. However," I paused, and went on mildly. "There's just one or two other points I'd like to clear up. Was Daniel called to give evidence?"

"Certainly not. A mere child. He was excused on grounds of his youth."

"And the good Canon Dingwall? Did he have any part in this affair? His name has never been mentioned, no, not once, and yet . . . somehow . . . I have an idea, one might say a suspicion, that his master mind . . . directed, shall we say, the strategy of your defense."

She had flushed angrily.

"The old Canon has always been a good friend to Danny and me, and he was a perfect godsend to us all through this ghastly misery . . . it's so like you, Carroll, to try to soil that relationship. Now get this straight. I've been persecuted enough. I'll take no more interrogations or cross-examinations from you. You can't do a thing about the case, it's closed, finished and done with."

"Naturally," I said. "But as you've been kind enough to supply the Matron with my past history I might well return the compliment with some of yours. She's a strict, straitlaced character. And while you didn't create that miraculous wind for her, I think you did imply, shall we say, natural causes. There was no mention of this strange fatality, the subsequent Inquiry, the split Jury. Indeed, I think I recollect hearing you sadly breathe those useful words, heart failure."

"Don't, Carroll. Don't do it. For if you try, I have the drop on you. I'll go to that professor of yours with your fake testimonials and have him accuse you before the Medical Council."

"You'll have to dig him up first."

It did not get through to her at first. Then she sat down suddenly, on the enamel kitchen chair. She was as white as the chair, even before I said:

"You don't think I'm a complete moron. To run

such a risk. He had been dead a full year before I wrote them."

I saw her breast fill up with a slow, painful breath which came out as a long, soundless sigh. A silence followed, during which an extraordinary feeling seeped through me. I felt sorry for her, an emotion evoked, or at least intensified, by her attitude. Where had I seen it before: the head slightly drooping, face half averted, her profile clearly lined against the window—the dark eyes deep set against a high cheekbone, the nose with the faintest upturn that had once struck a note of high audacity, the mouth drooping now, but still beautiful, the clear-cut defiant chin? Yes, she was still, or had again become, an attractive woman.

"Carroll." Speaking slowly she went on. "Let's make a deal . . . a nonaggression pact."

For a moment I was tempted. But no, Carroll, no. You're too wise a bird to be caught with chaff.

"It would never work," I said. "I'm sorry for you, Cathy. But you and I are natural antagonists. You've already been undermining my authority. All the time you'd get in my hair. You would interfere with my . . . my way of life."

"You mean the Swede?"

"Since you mention it, among other things, yes. Let's face it. You started this thing. I was ready and willing to welcome you, to be the best of friends. But from the minute you laid eyes on me at the airport you set out to wreck me."

"Not really, Carroll," she said, seriously. "Please believe me."

I ignored that and continued logically.

"Now I don't want to hurt you, although you've tried to hurt me. I just want you to realize this is no place for you, and go quietly home."

"Home?" The way she said it was enough.

"You must think of your boy. He's more ill than you imagine. But perhaps you don't trust me."

"I know you're a good liar, when it suits you."

I let that pass and went on:

"He'll soon need hospital treatment. But you don't seem to show much feeling for him."

"I never show what I feel now, it's safer."

I had said it all, yet she had a secret quality that baffled me. Without moving, her eyes still fixed and sad, she said:

"I can still wreck you, Carroll. I can have the last word. You're such a smartie I'm surprised you haven't tumbled to it sooner. But you will, Carroll, and that's why I've held it back. It's staring you in the face."

I did stare at her. What was she getting at? Nothing. I shook it off.

"Don't try on that old cliff-hanger. I know you."

"Do you? It's surprising, Carroll. You've chased women and slept with them most of your life, yet you don't in the least understand them." Her voice broke. "And, dear God, you've never understood me. Never. No, not ever."

There was a deeper silence. The sky had clouded and all at once a heavy spatter of hail hit the window. That is the way of it in the high Alps—weather changes so dramatic they shake you, fascinate you, half drown you. Suddenly I remembered the brat parked on the open terrace. I got up and moved toward the door. I would not say another word. I had settled the whole blasted business.

But as I went out, butting against a blast of hail, she said:

"I'm not going, Carroll. Never."

thirteen

THAT SAME EVENING in my room I poured myself a soothing kümmel and settled down to work things out. I had just made my routine visit to the ward with particular thoroughness, giving Garvey, the older of the ex-pleurisy cases, who was due to go home to-morrow, a going over. He was completely recovered, but from her little side room Matron's eye had been on me, and it was my policy now to recover lost ground and work in with her again. I had already washed out that first idea of dropping the *Herald* on her desk. She read English badly, Davigan would talk herself out of it in a dozen different ways—such a shock, the accident, could not bear to think, even to speak of it! No, it would not be conclusive, not the real clincher.

A hard case, that Davigan, she had ruffled me, put my back up. While giving nothing away, she had set me worrying, with her: "I can still wreck you, Carroll." What could she be getting at, not bluffing I was sure, she had something important in reserve, still held back from me. I was now convinced that she had delivered the fatal nudge. Up there, on the parapet, already sick to death of him and with the big drop below, almost waiting one might say, she had been struck by that sudden irresistible impulse which induced in the same second the reflex shove. In self-preservation he had grabbed at her, caught the sleeve of her dress which had torn away, then toppled. It was a simple positive equation. But I needed proof.

To stimulate cerebration, I took a slow sip of the kümmel, which is made from the best Swiss cherries with admirable results. Yes, the answer must lie in what might be named the Dingwall-Daniel alliance. Impossible though it seemed, an understanding appeared to exist between these two, or to be more specific, a secret, unrevealed or purposely suppressed, perhaps even a shred of vital evidence, bearing on the case. On the face of it, an absurd situation, an inconceivable hypothesis—involving two opposites—an aged canon of the church, steeped in virtue, desiccated by holiness, and a small boy, the son of the victim, no more than seven years old. Yet these two were intimates, the one as teacher, the other as pupil, a strong sense of interest and affection bound them closely. And more, from the boy's manner, his reticence to all my tentative approaches, there was evidence of a pledge, at least a given promise, not to reveal the secret.

The longer I brooded over this the more my curiosity grew, the more I realized I would never get the bare unvarnished truth until I had it from Daniel. And I wanted it badly. I couldn't force the boy in any way, but there were subtler ways of getting round him. And on this decision I finished the kümmel.

I knew I would not sleep easily with this on my mind so I went to my desk and dashed off a letter to Lotte explaining how busy I had been and how I hoped, and wanted, to see her, but for the time being must continue to toe the line of duty. I'd had two from her since she phoned, the second had been more than impatient. It was late when I sealed the envelope. I yawned, undressed, took a warm shower, and turned in. Even then I could not sleep. For once my phobia was not the trouble. Apart from the Davigan muddle, it was too long since I had been in Lotte's bed.

But next morning I was up, bright and early, consorting with Matron in the office and winning a brief nod of approval for my punctuality.

"You know that we send Garvey home today?" I said, after I had greeted her.

"*Jawohl.*" She gave me a queer look, charged with suspicion. "So you go once again to the airport?"

"No, Matron," I said, confidingly, almost endearingly. "I've had rather too much of that place lately. Garvey's a big boy, I'll put him on the train at Davos with his air ticket in his pocket and a tag in his buttonhole. All he has to do is walk across Zurich station to the air terminal. They know all about our Maybelle lot there."

"Ach so." She looked pleased, even gave me a half smile. "That I like besser for him . . ." adding significantly, "and for you, Herr Doktor." It was the second Herr Doktor I had that week.

"And if it's all right with you, Matron—you know I always consult you—I thought I would take Daniel along. It would be a nice change for him."

"So? You think him well enough for such?"

"You know what his future is, Matron." I presented her with my most humane expression. "Don't you feel he ought to have a little enjoyment in his short life, while he's having this good spell?"

"*Ja*, it is vell said. I agree." She nodded, and gave me that look again, the Hulda version of whimsey. "At least he keeps you from mischief, which is goot."

As might be expected, Davigan was busy in the kitchen, producing savory smells from a range of pots. Without disturbing her, I managed to get hold of Daniel who jumped at the unexpected prospect of the trip. We got into the Opel, Daniel and I in front, Garvey behind. He was a lumpy boy of fifteen from Edmonton, who never had much to say for himself. Since his pleural effusion had dried up he had put on weight, he looked well, and although incapable of expressing his thanks he was, I imagined, grateful for what we had done for him.

"Glad to be going home, Garvey?" I said, making conversation over my shoulder.

"So, so, sir." He almost whistled that one.

"You've missed your folks?"

"Well, I've missed the Spurs."

"Your what?"

"He means his football team. Tottenham Hotspurs," said the little knowall at my elbow.

We were at Davos in half an hour and after I had

put Garvey, well labeled, on the Zurich train, we had a hot chocolate at Zemmer's in the High Street, after which, as I'd planned, I took him to the big covered ice stadium. The hockey match between Villars and Davos had just begun.

I had thought he would enjoy it, but not all that much. He lapped it up, cheering the home team like the oldest inhabitant. After the fourth quarter, when we went out, he said:

"I wish I could skate like that, Dr. Laurence."

"Why not?"

He smiled and shook his head.

"I'm afraid chess will have to be my game."

"It is your game," I said heartily. "If you're still keen on that match at the Pfeffermühle I might put it on for you."

"Ah, yes," he said eagerly. "I would love that, absolutely."

"Let's make a date then," I said. "How about next Saturday?"

He began to laugh, in great spirits.

"May I look up my little book to see if I'm free?" Then broke off the joke. "No, seriously, that would be wonderful."

There's a restaurant in Davos called the Fluehgass, which is quiet and good. I took him there. Although the Grisons is a German-speaking canton the menu was promisingly typed in French, and after an amicable show of consulting my companion I decided on filet mignons *au bolets* with *pommes frites* and a cup of clear strong oxtail soup as a starter. You get tired of the eternal veal in Switzerland and that tender pink steak would be good for him. And I ordered a half bottle of the Val d'Or Johannesburger, a light delicious wine from Sion. One glass wouldn't hurt him.

"This is very cozy." He rubbed his hands. It was a good corner booth, near the pine log that was smoldering on the fieldstone hearth.

We were getting chummier than ever, as I had planned. It was too easy and I didn't dislike it. Although he might be a little toad, he was well mannered, never bored or nagged you and knew when to be silent.

He lapped up the soup and on the first chew of the filet, rolled his eyes at me.

"Try a sip of the wine."

He did.

"That's delicious too. Like nippy honey. Good job Matron isn't looking, Dr. Laurence."

"Why don't you drop the Doctor," I suggested. "Just make it Laurence."

He stopped eating.

"What a compliment."

"To me or you?"

"To me, of course." And looking up, he gave me a warm, diffident smile.

It hit me, that smile, right smack between the eyes. Where had I seen it before? In some old cracked snapshot, or mirrored faintly in a long forgotten past. Smile now, dear, and look at the camera. Or, as I grinned in the looking glass, admiring my new school cap. My smile, before the early gloss had worn off me.

I felt void, sick and shaken. God, it was the moment of truth all right. Why hadn't I rumbled it before? She had told me it was staring me in the face—the AB blood group should have warned me—almost a natural follow on from a group O father. But I had got out of so many beds scot-free, I never dreamed that I had balled up the issue in that first one. And Davigan had waited, ready to spring it on me when the time came, holding it, nursing it along for the knockout. That rattled me. Did she expect me to fall on her bosom and weep? Soft music and the young lovers reunited at last. If so, what a hope. I wasn't the type to swoon and melt. I would work something out, I would . . .

"Are you feeling all right, Laurence?"

I pulled myself together. He was looking at me with concern.

"I'm fine." After all, he wasn't to blame. "Just something . . . something that went the wrong way."

No words of mine were ever more truly spoken.

With the help of black coffee and a brandy I got through the rest of the meal. Then it was time to take off.

As on the night of our meeting I made him lie down on the back seat of the car. I wanted no chatter, and he needed the rest. The meal had made him sleepy. I drove slowly all the way home, scarcely aware of the twists and turns of that difficult road, staring straight ahead.

The thought that I was co-proprietor of this derelict little property in the back seat, this sad little freak, of frail physique and precocious intellect, the bright brain in the dim body, was a crusher, all right. Take it from me—a crusher.

Yet as I drove on, blind, reason began to assert itself. A crusher? But why, Carroll? Why? Don't be so hasty, counting yourself out, when you're not even in the ring. All this is past history. Long past. I swerved instinctively on a bend, missing the other car by an inch, barely seeing it. Yes, the book is closed and can't be reopened. Who saw you turn back that night of the ordination and go skulking . . . well, let's be polite and say speeding, toward the Considine house? Only the Almighty, and He is unlikely to broadcast it from the heavens. And were you not welcomed? You were, Carroll. Warmly welcomed. And afterwards, while you remained in total ignorance she accepted her responsibility, married Davigan, covered up the situation, lived with it. Who is to believe her at this late stage of the game if she tries to pin the blame on you? Can you see her going to Hulda: "Excuse me, Matron, there's something I forgot to tell you, just escaped my memory, so to speak . . . the truth is that . . ." She's wearing a shawl and it's snowing outside. What a B picture! She couldn't do it ever, she is too . . . too tough. She would know it must get the horse's laugh. No, Carroll, don't rush in where angels fear to tread. I liked that touch—it made me smile. Yes, say nothing, play it sostenuto, and await developments, if any. Meanwhile, on your side of the fence, keep after the kid for further revelations.

I felt somewhat better, relieved in fact, after this

self-communion, and by the time we'd reached the Maybelle I was able to face the Matron, who had been waiting on us, with my usual self-possession.

"So, you are safe home again, Daniel. Was it a goot time?"

"Splendid, thank you, Matron." I stood by while he sketched our program for her.

"Ach, so." She turned to me, looking pleased. "And he seems not too tired?"

"I was extremely careful," I said soberly, encouraged by her manner which was mild, even remotely kindly —perhaps Davigan had been laying off me at last.

"Well, now it is for you the bed," said Hulda, taking his ever-ready hand. "Come. Your mother shops in the village so I vill put you." Looking over her shoulder as they went out: "Hot coffee in your flask, Herr Doktor."

It wouldn't last of course, I felt in all my bones there must be stormy weather ahead, but for the present I almost felt a member of the family.

fourteen

TOWARD THE END of the week the thermometer had risen and on Saturday, under a gray and humid sky, the *Föhn* was stirring, that soft damp neurotic wind detested by the Swiss. There are two winds in Switzerland, the *bise* which blasts down Lac Leman to Geneva and chills you to the bone, and the *Föhn* which on occasion blows everywhere and is worse than the *bise*, reducing you to a wet sweat rag, wrung out and limp. Around the Maybelle patches of soiled snow despoiled the landscape, slush glued up the streets and a steady drip came from the suffering pines. In short, a horrible day, but one well suited to our purpose. Without a doubt, this Saturday afternoon all the habitués would be parked round the stove drying themselves out at the Pfeffermühle.

Looking him over that morning I was less inclined now to go through with my promise, indeed, if I had known the living hell that would be let loose on me that same evening I would have cut out the entire affair. But Daniel had not allowed me to forget it, and in fact I had my own purpose behind the expedition. This afternoon when I had indulged the kid with his chess I meant to coax out of him the one last bit of information I needed. So when he'd had his rest after the *Mittagessen* I smuggled him into the station wagon and took off quietly. At the worst I could tell Matron we had gone for a drive. As for Davigan, we were now barely on speaking terms. He'd had a sleep and was in his usual chatty mood, grateful that I was taking him and a bit excited.

He was not on the uplift now, though still bearing up, just a trifle shimmery—his red cells rather better than when I first made the count, but these infernal whites creeping up on him again. By exerting myself I had become even more chummy with him.

"I hope I don't let you down, Laurence," he said, as the car slushed through the village.

"Don't give it a thought. Just enjoy your game."

"Oh, I will. I love a good stiff contest."

"I'm sorry I'm so little use to you. One of the advantages of going back home, you'll resume your games with Dingwall."

"Yes . . . I suppose so," he said, rather doubtfully.

I drew up and parked at the Pfeffermühle where an array of old bicycles, the form of transport favored by the locals, indicated a full house. We went in, greeted by a waft of odorous steamy air and a general exhalation of "grüssgotts." The Maybelle, as I have mentioned, not without pride, was in good standing with the village, an esteem which, perhaps because their knowledge of me was slight, I appeared to share. I took the table at the window, furthest from the stove, which was red-hot, and ordered a beer and an apfelsaft. Yes, as far as I could judge, they were all there: Bemmel, the man we were after, ex-teacher and leader of the troupe; Schwartz the water bailiff; Minder the undertaker, not busy today; a couple of nearby peasant farmers; and of course Bachmann, owner of the tavern, together with a fair congregation of the usual village hangers-on.

Bemmel, though a man of some learning, which explained his prestige with the group, was a weird piece of work. Extremely short and thick, uncouth, untidy and unbelievably hairy, with an all-enveloping, yellow-stained beard that left only his two small sharp eyes exposed, he might have passed for the original beatnik or the oldest of the Three Dwarfs. He wore a soiled knitted brown cardigan and skullcap, a half-smoked unlit cigar end protruding from its hairy nest. This half burned-out stub, well masticated, held for hours between the jaws, is in the rural cantons, the prestige symbol of the Swiss male. Thus equipped, and with the colored cantonal skullcap well set back on his head, he may undertake the most menial tasks, shovel snow or muck, spread liquid manure with the hose between his legs, disembowel the dung heap or handle the *glockenspiel*, yet remain a free man, a voter, which the women are not, a true upstanding Swiss, consciously aware of himself as the lineal descendant of the mythical Wilhelm Tell.

A marked silence had followed our arrival, they had

175

their eyes on us, inclined to welcome our intrusion as a diversion on a dull day. I waited until our drinks were brought then casually asked for chessmen and the board, a request which seemed to stir them up. Once we had set up the men and begun to play, beyond a few desultory remarks made simply as a cover for their self-esteem, they were watching us closely.

For reasons of strategy, since I wished to avoid the obvious, I did my best but, as usual, our game ended in short order, which gave me the opportunity to make a public exhibition of myself.

"*Verflixt! Gopfriedstutz!* Everytime he wins." I threw it at them in loud, angry Schweizerdeutsch.

This caught their fancy and Bemmel, who was stuck on his French and liked to show it off, said indulgently:

"*Il est bon, le petit?*"

"*Bon! C'est un génie. En Écosse il est champion de sa ville.*"

"*Et vous dites qu'il gagne toujours?*" The cigar end looked amused.

I thought it time to bring in the others.

"*Niemand kann gegen diesen Kerl gewinnen,*" I said it in Schweizerdeutsch, and continued in the same crude lingo. "And I prove it. For a round of drinks I back him against the best man here." It would be worth the money just to drag in Bemmel.

There was silence followed by a sudden cackle. In a minute they were all bursting themselves.

"You can laugh," I said. "But will you play? You, Herr Bemmel? You accept my bet?"

This dried up the laughter but not the grins. They were all looking at Bemmel.

"Ach, Herr Doktor, we cannot refuse your so generous hospitality. Perhaps I give your leetle friend a short lesson."

He got up, stretched, still grinning, then waddled over and took my place. The gang grouped themselves back of him while, after a preliminary of setting up the pieces, he made a condescending gesture.

"Pegin then, leetle poy."

"Oh, no. We must be fair. You are the challenger. You have the honor and may have the white."

Although I did not know this, apparently white always starts first.

With a hand like a ham the schoolmaster made the initial move, a knight. Daniel replied with a pawn. I was wishing by now, wishing like mad, that I had a real knowledge of the game beyond my usual incentive of trying to knock off my opponent's queen. I knew that Daniel must lose, banked on it in fact, to soften him up. But with the thing begun, I wanted him to put up a good show and the devil of it was, I couldn't follow the technique of the game. All I could do was watch the faces of the players.

Daniel was pale but calm, the schoolmaster still wearing his cigar end jauntily, making his moves quite fast and, after the fourth, sounding a helpful confidential warning.

"Achtung, leetle poy!" He was worse than Hulda.

Whatever happened in the next few moves was beyond me but it seemed that, after two pawns were exchanged for a bishop that Daniel calmy sacrificed, the butt came in for some harsh mastication and instead of the *achtung* we had an "*Ach so*" followed by a measurable pause. Something had gone wrong with that quick and sudden *coup*.

After that the pace was slower. Bemmel in particular took his time, punctuating his moves with aggressive grunts in different keys. Background noises from the spectators accompanied the various moves. Unlike me, they knew the game, and were watching it, waiting for the kill. Daniel remained silent, paler than before, but gradually a few beads of moisture began to break on his brow. This sign of concentration, or of stress, had me worried, and I blamed myself for letting him in for it. Worse followed when the schoolmaster moved his queen, gave out a thick chuckle, and lay back in his seat, supported by a chorus of approval from the rear.

"Czechk."

I thought: it's the beginning of the end. But no, not yet. Daniel moved out of check then sacrificed a rook that had been threatened by the queen, Bemmel removed it with a grin. Daniel moved his remaining bishop. Then came a hollow pause. A hint of surprise had crept into the assembly, they were muttering.

"*Achtung; der Bauer,* Bemmel!"

The bishop moved again, two further moves, then Daniel slid forward an inconspicuous but nasty little pawn. At least Bemmel did not appear to love it. And there was more noise from the background, but differently attuned.

"Grossartig, mit dem Bauer spielt er den Ruy Lopez. Die Dame ist bedroht."

I was watching Bemmel now. He moved restlessly, shifting his position to lean forward, peering hard at the board. Finally he lay back and with a forced grin and an attempt at bonhomie exclaimed:

"You defend yourself well. I think we agree it is *nul*."

A low rumble of dissent came from the followers which seemed to indicate an honest note of warning.

"Nein, nein, mein Lieber."

It was unnecessary.

"You want me to concede a draw? I'm afraid I must refuse. But if you wish I will permit you to resign."

"Ach, nein, nein!" Bemmel grunted.

After a long, long pause which would never have been permitted by a time clock, the schoolmaster, his brow furrowed by confused concentration and the beginnings of anguish, moved a defensive pawn. It was taken by the same bishop.

"Ach, so . . . Wieder der Bauer." Bachmann had left his counter and was craning his neck in the background.

Two other moves followed, slow, extremely slow, from Bemmel, who was sweating now all down the back of his neck, very fast and confident from Daniel. And that was it.

"Checkmate."

A stupefied silence; it had happened so quickly. Then a burst of genuine applause. I thought Bemmel had swallowed the cigar, but he tore it out of its nest and flung it at the stove where it stuck and started to hiss

179

at him. Thus disarmed, he was no longer a free and virile Swiss but a poor stuttering fool. Impossible to see his face, but the beard seemed definitely bloodshot. "*Ach so, ach so,*" he kept repeating. "*Ein glückliches Stück.*"

"Yes," said Daniel, picking up the meaning. "I was very lucky. You played splendidly." And he held out his hand.

I didn't like the kid for that—he was back in his Lord Fauntleroy role, you'd think I had just entered him for Eton, but I must admit it went over big with the gang. It seemed appropriate to celebrate. I called for the drinks.

For the next ten minutes we had a regular party. I did not let it go on any longer. When the excitement began to subside I got up and, to promote good feeling, paid the score. This seemed to help Bemmel, who managed a dim smile. I hoped it might lower his blood pressure. Still brooding, he was feeling around for the stub, wondering where it had got to, and beginning to think up excuses. But we had wrecked him, he would never be the same again. *Le petit Écossais* would become a legend at the Pfeffermühle.

When we left they saw us to the car, and every good Schweizer one of them, even Bemmel, shook hands with the kid before they waved us off. I drove slowly, taking the long way home.

"You put on a good show," I said.

"Not really, Laurence." He laughed. He was brimming over. "You see, he tried to scholar's mate me right away. It put him at such a disadvantage. I went straight into a reverse Ruy Lopez and against that, the Sicilian game that he put on was no use. You noticed those last moves, didn't you, P–B5, P–B6, B–Kt2?"

I nodded, to please him.

"Poor man, I'm afraid he was very upset."

"It'll do him good. He's always been a bit of a blowhard. They don't really go for him back there."

"He's quite good, really, and could beat me the next time. I don't always win you know, Laurence, in spite of what you said, but I did want to, for your sake." He looked up at me. "Not to let you down, you know."

Now he was at his worst again. He had just won the Wall Game with the first goal in twenty years. But I put up with it.

"How do you make out against the old Canon?" I asked, working toward my objective.

"He's beaten me several times, especially at the beginning."

"He taught you?"

"Yes, and lots of other things."

"You like him?"

"Well, naturally."

"You know, Daniel," I manufactured a sigh, "I'm rather jealous of that old bag of bones. You're so very close to him. I keep thinking of that private understanding you share with him. In a way it worries me."

"Oh, it needn't," he said quickly. "If anyone, I should worry."

"Then why don't you let me in on it?" It griped me to say this, but I had to get what I wanted. "I might be able to help."

There was a silence. The warmth had gone out of his face. He looked deflated. At last he said, slowly:

"I have become very attached to you, Laurence. In fact if I didn't know how much you hate sissy stuff, I could put it much stronger. But I've absolutely given my word not to speak of a certain thing."

The nudge that sent Davigan over! He could mean nothing else. He was there; he had seen it. I wanted almost unbearably to know the truth.

"Come on, Danny boy. We're such pals now. No one would ever know."

"I can't." He shook his head sadly yet firmly. A sober pause followed, then his expression cleared as though he saw a way out. "However, if you guessed it by yourself there would be no harm. It would let me out, for I still wouldn't have told you." He added: "I might even be allowed to give you a little hint. You're so clever it might help you."

"Let's have it then." I couldn't bear this. We were almost at the Maybelle, turning into the drive.

"That same afternoon, when the Canon came out with me to the convent door, he sat up in his wheelchair, tapped me on the shoulder, and said:

"Silence is golden."

I stared at him, stupefied. Was he having me on? Impossible. Yet what a letdown. I could have clipped him on his aggravating little pan.

"Out," I said, drawing up with a jerk at the front porch, "and for God's sake don't give the women any hints we were in the pub."

When I had dropped him off I garaged the car with

a violence that reflected my mood. After all my careful planning, my staging of the chess match, all this build-up, I was left with nothing but a three-word prissy proverb from the kindergarten copybook: "Silence is golden!" The sleet was coming down again.

fifteen

THAT EVENING, after I had locked up, I sat up late in
my room tippling kümmel, going over that blasted
riddle: *Silence is golden.* What a cliché! Was it
merely an injunction from Dingwall, meaning keep
your trap shut? Yet the phrase was the last to be expected from a man of such incisive mind. It belonged
with such lollypops as A stitch in time saves nine, or,
Don't count your chickens before they're hatched. Of
course, he was using it toward a child. No, no, that
wouldn't work, not with that juvenile brain trust. Certainly the *command* existed: silence, don't talk! Yet
there must be another, and a hidden implication, possibly in the word *golden.* An idea occurred to me:
could this be a reference, jocular, no doubt, to the
half-crown tip given by Dingwall at that precise moment, to ensure cooperation? Nonsense. I dismissed it
as totally out of key with either character. Yet golden
suggested money, wealth, some precious thing. But
nothing could be more apparent than that Davigan had

no money. I knew for a certainty that the widow hadn't a stiver. I had seen Matron slipping a few francs into her purse before she came back with that new pair of snow boots.

I gave up at last, locked the bottle in its cupboard, undressed, and as an afterthought, washed out the glass so that no incriminating evidence should go back to Hulda. Shortly after midnight I fell asleep.

It seemed less than an hour before I awoke with a start. Someone was banging on my window. I stumbled up and opened it to be met by a blast of sleet through which I dimly saw Davigan, in her dressing gown, bareheaded, hair blown by the wind, with a wild look about her.

"Come, quickly. Daniel's taken ill."

"What's the matter?" I had to shout. "Stomach upset?"

"No. A bleeding. Hurry. Please hurry. He looks dreadfully ill."

Make no bones about it, she seemed half out of her mind. I waved her away, banged the casement shut. I could never find that light switch in the dark, but I did at last, buttoned on my pants, pulled a sweater over my pajama jacket, shoved my feet into slippers, picked up the emergency case that always stood in the hall, and unbolted the front door.

It was a hell of a night, gale force wind and heavy sleet. I cursed myself for forgetting my raincoat. I was well soaked before I reached the chalet.

All the lights were on. She had left the door open. I went in. He was lying on his bunk, flat on his back, collapsed, shrunk into himself, totally blanched. No palpable pulse. He didn't know I was there.

"How did this come on?" I was opening my bag in a hurry.

"He had diarrhea, went to the bathroom." She was shivering all over. "I left it for you to see."

I put my head round the bathroom door. One look was enough—the curse of myelocytic leukemia is the liability to massive hemorrhages. He must be practically exsanguine. As I broke an ampul of camphor in oil and charged the hypodermic, I said:

"Get some clothes on, or a coat, for God's sake, and run round and knock up Matron. The side door's unlocked."

He didn't apparently respond to the injection but now there was just the hint of a carotid pulse. I took the extra blanket from the end of the bed, spread it, and rolled him on it. Double wrapped, he was practically weightless as I carried him across the courtyard into the little side room off the ward. Davigan had pulled on a coat and the new snow boots and gone ahead of me.

So now what? Ever since that first glance at him I had been cursing myself. I knew I should have laid in at least a temporary blood bank for him. Apart from my own knowledge Lamotte had stressed this precaution. Being what I am, I had put it off, passed it up, or plain forgotten. An immediate transfusion was what he must have and the only way was for me both to perform it and act as donor.

Though stinkingly sentimental, this was a plain necessity. It sounds simple. Perhaps you have lain at ease, feeling praiseworthy and benevolent, while the nurse drew off and bottled your 350 cc's before you knew it, then ushered you in sweetly to coffee and biscuits in the cafeteria. This was going to be a double act, and quite different. I had only the barest equipment, nothing prepared, and the patient, with practically no penetrable veins, was in extremis.

"He still is bleeding?"

Hulda had appeared, in silence for once, and unbelievably in full uniform. Never had I been so glad to see her.

"He's about lost it all," I said. "We must let him have it back at once."

"But how?"

"I'm universal type O and he's group AB. Let's make the shift quick as we can. There's a vacuum transfusion flask in the surgery emergency cupboard. Bring it now."

"I already look." She did not move. "Someone is taking things from that cupboard. It is perhaps broken, at least no longer there."

I was too shaken even to swear.

This was the final crusher. These vacuum flasks, treated with an anticoagulant, sodium citrate, or better, heparin, and capped with thin rubber to take the needle puncture, are essential intermediate receptacles in standard practice. I had meant to fill it from my own brachial vein, suspend it high on the stand and transfuse. Now, if at all, it had to be direct and I knew the full meaning of that word. Useless to attempt direct transfusion from my vein to his—the venous pressure was insufficient. He needed arterial pressure and arterial blood.

All this passed through my mind in a flash, and Hulda must have read it in my face. Why ever had I tried to make a cod of her? The old battle-ax was a regular standby, calm, efficient, experienced. In four minutes, while I took his blood pressure—it was less than fifteen—she had collected, sterilized and assembled the tubing, cannula and needles—primitive equipment by Kantonspital standards, but it would work. She put her hand on a chair, even got a towel to dry the worst of the rain off me, then said:

"You vish to sit?"

I shook my head. We'd get a better flow if I stood.

"Just tighten the tourniquet on his upper arm."

Now we were off. I bent forward to insert the needle. The tourniquet should have brought up the brachial vein by interrupting the venous flow, but there was no flow and no vein. I felt, and felt again. Nothing. I began to sweat. Over the years in practice there are some skills you acquire and some that will always be beyond you. Ignoring my deficiencies, I had at least this ability: for a sad six months, running a VD clinic in Plymouth, taking Wasserman specimens and giving intravenous Salvarsan, I must have pierced hundreds of veins, until I could do it, first time, clean as a whistle, in my sleep. And now, when I needed it, I was stuck.

"I'll have to incise and go into the jugular."

She already had the lancet. He was too far gone to

feel the incision I made in his neck. His eyes, glazed like the eyes of a dead fish, stared glassily toward the ceiling. And finally there it was, thin as a bird's windpipe. I inserted the cannula, then with my one free hand I simply broke the cord of my pajama pants and let them drop with my trousers. Holding the other needle tight between my thumb and second finger I felt with my free forefinger for the big throb, just below the inguinal canal. I had it. Finally, with the unspoken thought: this is it! I plunged the needle deep and laterally into my right femoral artery. I knew at once I had hit the big artery of the leg, the shock ran all through me.

I kept it going, controlling the tube between my finger and thumb. I didn't want to choke him up at the start. After a long moment the Matron said:

"It does vell, Herr Doktor." She had a finger on his left carotid. "The pulse begins."

The change, if you had not seen it before, or perhaps you would not wish to, was spectacular. He began to lose that shrunken look, to fill out and gain color like an inflated breath-test balloon. The pulse in his neck was quite visible now and his lungs were making up for lost time. Then his eyes flickered and he looked straight at me.

It gave me the damndest, silliest feeling I had ever had in my entire life. I wanted to burst myself, laughing at myself. Carroll, the sob sister's dream. What a squirt, standing there, completely debagged, leaning against the table for support, pants tangled around the ankles, the personal article dangling visible and loose.

How in the name of everything correct and proper had I ever landed myself in such a clownish situation? Only because it was my fate to be wrong-way Carroll. My unlucky star, with a devilish sense of humor, had arranged it for me. I could not escape it. That was my one alibi that saved me from being a creep. I hated it worse when Hulda said:

"Oh, it is so goot, *er ist viel besser.*"

As I didn't answer, she asked, hurriedly:

"But he vill bleed again?"

"He's getting enough healthy platelets to clot everything for weeks."

Actually, I was beginning to feel slack at the knees, but to punish myself and because I wanted no repeat of this performance, I would give him the full quota.

"I think now he goes straight asleep." Hulda breathed it into my left earhole.

Probably the alcohol still in my blood from the kümmel was sending him over. Do him good too, the little rat. Better ease this over with Matron.

"I took a simple hypnotic before turning in, he's probably got a trace of it."

"Goot."

It had to end sometime. He'd had more than enough now and was fast asleep. I disconnected, at the cost of another femoral spasm, put two fine stitches in his neck incision. He barely moved. Matron had everything ready and without blinking an eye at my private possessions, carefully and firmly taped the puncture on my leg. Then she settled him in the bed and covered him up. I didn't want to see him again for years.

"Now I go tell the poor mother all is vell."

"Do that," I said. "But don't let her disturb him."

"I return quickly."

Now I was glad to sit down. I shut my eyes and rested my head on one hand. I felt light on top, as though I had emptied my brains into him. Not that he needed them. Matron was back.

"Ach, she has such relief, poor voman. But you must take her alzo a sleeping pill, or surely she vill not rest."

"Okay," I said, giving the stupidest affirmative in Christendom. It shows how low I felt.

"Now I make you some coffee."

I refused it.

"I want to sleep too."

I stood up. She was between me and the door. I couldn't avoid it when she took my hand. What's the matter with you, Carroll, everyone wants to hold your hand?

"Herr Doktor." She drew a deep breath. "I think . . . I know I misjudge you. That was a most fine action."

There it comes again. Green lights and soft music. Carroll, the blood-giving hero, pride of the comic strip.

The old battle-ax was killing me. She kept watching me like a mother hen as I got a couple of sodium Amytal capsules out of my bag—those red and green knockouts.

"Good-night," I said.

"*Gute Nacht, mein lieber Herr Doktor.*"

sixteen

As I STRUGGLED across the courtyard against the wind the village clock struck two, the sound muffled by the driving sleet. In the chalet a single window showed a narrow rectangle of light. I went in, without knocking, in a hurry. I needed sleep, and meant to make this short.

She was seated on the edge of her bed, in her thin, cheap dressing gown, bent forward, half supporting herself with an elbow on her knee. Although she had shed the coat and the wet nightdress, she still had on the snow boots.

"I've brought you a couple of sleeping pills."

She came out of her thoughts with a start. Beyond that she did not move or speak. I went over and gave them to her. At least she let me put them in her free hand. A bottle was standing on the dressing table. I saw the special clinic mark on it, the big copying ink: M.B.

"Stolen from the store cupboard," I said.

"How else would I get it?" she said dully, adding an afterthought. "You know I'm broke. And God knows I'm not a drunk, but just like yourself, Carroll, I need a drink occasionally. I did tonight."

I could agree with her there. She had that broken-down look about her I had noticed when she first arrived, but now there was no fight in her. It bothered me.

"Don't take the pills then. Brandy and the barbiturates don't mix."

"Who cares?" She sipped the brandy, it was neat.

There was a silence.

"I suppose I ought to thank you."

"Save it. I'm going to bed."

"Couldn't you do with a drink? On the house."

I hesitated. I felt all in, the walls of the room had begun to tilt, and the label on the bottle said Martell's 3 Stars.

"In your own interests," I said, when I had fetched a tumbler from the bathroom, "don't let your pal the Matron see this bottle. She already has strong suspicions in your direction. By the way, did you knock over a glass flask when you were pilfering?"

"Yes. I heard someone coming. It broke."

So what? I merely said: "I'd forget that, if I were you."

The cognac was good. The only chair was occupied by her wet coat, hung over the back to dry. I sat down on the bed. She was so unnaturally silent and depressed I had to know why.

"What's biting you, Davigan?"

She did not answer for a minute.

"For one thing I've just realized how ill Daniel is."

"You care?"

"You think I don't?"

"On the evidence, I think you're a pretty well-seasoned character, Davigan."

"What evidence, Carroll?"

"Circumstantial."

"Because I don't whimper and weep? I've stoppered up my feelings so long it's become a habit not to show them."

Was it the brandy? We were mugging it like a couple of cross-talk comedians. It had to stop.

"Let's just say: You've had a rough passage, Davigan, and it shows."

There was a pause, then she said:

"Have it your way, Carroll. Your trouble is you only think the worst of people."

"I've only seen the worst."

"That's all you've ever looked for." And she gave me a long sad look that made me drop my eyes. Naturally I lamped her big ridiculous boots.

"Why don't you take off those blasted snow boots? You look so damn pathetic in them," I shouted, and pushing her back, I made a double swoop, unzippered them, and tore them off.

Upended like this, lying back, with her knees up and apart and her thin wrapper flung open, she gazed up at me with such a look of silent pleading and half-frightened appeal, it hit me like a bomb. Everything seemed to happen instinctively and at once, and we were in bed under the blanket, her arms were locked around me, and her terribly wet tears running down my cheek.

"You said you never wept, Cathy," I whispered.

"This is my one big chance."

No one will ever get the record of these next long moments. Why should I pander to dirty minds like mine, and foul up what was certainly to that date the sweetest and, in the aftermath, the strangest experience of my slightly soiled life? The more so, since it might induce the false and pernicious hope that all was now set for a happy and sentimental reunion. Yet it is permissible to state that afterwards her arms still held me, as mine held her. She had no desire to free herself, roll over, and light a cigarette, until lust promoted another essay. Nor had I. Restful and at peace we still belonged to each other, united by the act, and grateful to one another. All frustration, all antagonism dissolved, there was in her a softness I would never have believed existed, nothing kept back in her response, a total surrender. Let's be cynical and use Lotte's jeering phrase: it was heart to heart, and roses round the door.

She sighed at last, not releasing me.

"Why didn't we make a go of it, Laurie? It's all been such a misery and a mess." I couldn't stop her, she went on. "Davigan knew Daniel wasn't his. Did he ever let me forget it? Poor man, I suppose it was hard for him too. He knew why I took him. Oh, if only you'd answered my letter."

"What letter?"

"The one I wrote to the ship."

"I never had that letter," I said slowly, and it was the God's truth.

"How can I believe you, Laurie? You're such a terrible liar, darling. But I love you, I always have, and heaven help me I always will. You know what, darling?"

"No," I said.

"Everything stems from that afternoon when we were kids in the woods. I've thought of it so often. Have you?" Had I not? "That frustration . . . at the very moment . . . it set us against one another, made us fight each other."

"Hark at the little Krafft-Ebing!"

"It's true. Let's not quarrel any more, Laurence. You're so sweet when you try."

"Shall I try again?"

"Don't desecrate it, Laurie. This isn't just sex. I love you from my heart."

And she did, with all the rest too, snuggling to me afterwards and saying sleepily:

"Don't make me get up, love. That was always the worst. Creeping into that cold toilet like a drab."

How warm and comfortable and soft she was, her arms still round me. As she began to breathe deeply and quietly I felt myself sinking down, down into a sound and blissful sleep.

seventeen

About a hundred years later I woke with a start. It must have been at least a hundred years for I felt that old. I was on my left side and a soft arm lay across my chest. With an effort I dismembered my wrist from the blankets and squinted at my watch. Ten minutes after nine. Not possible. But it was, and bright daylight glared in the room. Bright daylight and a cold in-draught of air. Had that awakened me? I turned, with an effort, and there, with the open door behind her, unbelieving horror spread across her face, was the Matron.

No, not a vision of the night, but sordid reality. The ultimate humiliating discovery on the morning after, the joke of the music hall comedian, the lowest form of bedroom farce. What the butler saw! You could churn it out for a copper, turning the handle of the antique slot machine on some half-rotting pier.

I did not find it amusing. My start had roused the

third member of the party and for a long, long moment a painful silence bore down on the room.

"You vill come to my office in one hour." Hulda finally let this command go at me.

Moving to the dressing table, she picked up the brandy bottle, turned, and went out, holding it away from her like a hand grenade. The bang of the door shook the chalet, like an explosion.

"Oh, God. I'm sorry, Carroll."

"Yes," I said. "We can't laugh this one off."

I got out of bed slowly. She was before me. "Just give me a few minutes and I'll make your breakfast. Do let me, Carroll, I want to so much. There's Nescafé and eggs and fresh bread in the kitchen. You need it, Carroll."

"I'd better not stay."

She saw that I meant it.

While she watched me with concern, I began to drag on my garments. My joints creaked. The puncture in my leg was a permanent stitch. I felt myself a fully qualified candidate for the A.H.V. which, if you're unfamiliar with these symbols, is the Swiss Old Age Pension.

"What'll happen?"

"The worst."

"I'm sorry, dear," she said again, her hands still pressed together. "I love you and bring you nothing but harm."

I went across to my room.

No coffee, no croissants, no fresh fruit on the sideboard. Deprived of these reviving elements, my spirits sagged lower. I would have given a lot for a sup of that cognac. I only had the kümmel and the thought of that sugary draught was enough. I could have done with a good hot shower but I was already dressed. I brushed my teeth, not looking at myself in the glass, then shaved by the sense of touch. Naturally I nicked my chin. Now I had to look. More blood, I thought— it was watery and thin. When I'd finally made the cotton wool stick, I went out.

First I had to see the *fons et origo*, the cause of all my trouble. He was sitting up in bed, washed, brushed and looking better than new. What else could you expect? All those rotten deceased white cells drained out of him and all that healthy blood pumped in. He was bursting with my red blood corpuscles. Just for the moment he was a brand new little bastard. I could have killed him.

"Good morning, Laurence. I've been longing for you to come. How are you?"

"*Wunderbar.* How are you?"

"*Wunderbar* also. I'm feeling terribly fit. And I've just had a lovely breakfast from Matron."

"Tell me."

"Cereal and cream, soft poached egg and a glass of lovely pear juice."

"You're making me hungry."

The pocket chess was there, on the side table by the bed.

"How is the game going?"

"Matron wouldn't let me set it out on my knees. Not yet. So visually I'm replaying the one with Herr

Bemmel. I see now where I could have used a better fifth move: Kt to Q7."

"Careful," I said. "Don't let Bemmel win this one."

"Oh, this time I'm going to let him, just for fun."

"How's the little scratch on your neck?"

"Oh, fine." He looked at me archly. "Perhaps I cut myself shaving?"

"Yes," I said sourly. "Let's say you've had a close shave." This was moderately witty for me, on such a morning, but he missed the point. He had no idea of what he had been through. I took his pulse.

"Have your insides moved this morning?"

"Yes. Matron said it was quite normal."

Matron was well in on this act now.

"Well, take it easy. I'll see you later."

"Please, Laurence. And . . . I know how you hate what you call slop . . . but thank you for everything."

While I was at it, I dragged myself round the ward. Sheer cowardice, of course, putting off the evil moment. Young Higgins, the synovitis case, had completely healed and could go home with the ex-pleurisy, the Jamieson girl, any day now, which would leave more room for the Christmas holiday lot. But why make Christmas arrangements, Carroll? You'll not be here then, dear boy. I summoned up the blood, what was left of it, knocked at Matron's door.

"*Herein.*"

I went in.

She was at her desk, sitting up straight, waiting on me.

This office was smaller than mine and furnished with

her own things, surprisingly feminine—strange, I never thought of her as a woman, to me, despite the milk bars, she was sexless. Two finely worked samplers hung on the wall—how had she ever found time to stitch them?—and between them an old group photograph, row upon row of young nurses, already shapelessly garbed in white, novices of the night vigil—was she among them? She liked flowers and at the window, today, a fine pot of yellow chrysanthemums caught my gaze as, instinctively, it swiveled away from her.

"*Sitzen*," she said, pointing to a chair. I sat. She looked me over. Already I had lost control of the interview.

"Never," she went on, "never in all my life, have I had such shock, such horror. To behave zo, while that dear chile, zo ill, was sleeping."

I studied the chrysanthemums in silence. They were the fine feathery variety that cost money.

"And with the mother, too, which makes it most hateful of all."

Even though she slaughtered the syntax, she did make it sound pretty low. And for an instant I thought of coming clean and throwing the whole works at her. But no, that would not help. She would never believe me. That's the worst of trifling with the truth. When you recite the Lord's prayer they think you're kidding them.

"To spoil such fine vork of that evening with such bad morality," she went on feelingly. "Are you not ashamed?"

"I might be, Matron," I said humbly, "if I wasn't so hungry."

She gave me another long look, then banged the little hand bell on her desk. The probationer came in, big-eyed, too scared to look at me. Had she been listening at the door?

"Bring café crème and a croissant."

I could scarcely believe my ears. Was there, could there be, a gleam of hope, or was this merely the last wish of the condemned man?

"*Ja*," she said, reading my surprise. "You do not deserve. And at first I am zo angry I begin a letter to the committee."

She broke off. The coffee and the crescent had arrived on a tray. They must have been ready and waiting by the stove. I balanced it on the arm of the chair and dunked the crescent.

"But presently I think besser. Perhaps it is not all blame for you. For a man such a thing is perhaps necessary, even forgivable. You see, although I am *alt und gross*, I understand vell the men and their neets." With one eye half closed she gave me a knowing look with just the suggestion of a leer, as if she had just read through the Kinsey Report. It would have been comic if it had not been so fortunate for me. Yet perhaps she did know. Perhaps some dirty old Swiss doctor had seduced her when she was a probationer. No, impossible, she was completely, inviolably virginal.

She took a sharp breath between her teeth and continued:

"But for her, that voman, with all her pretending

to goodness and the husbant zo soon dead, it is a great sin, a crime, a falseness."

"But surely, Matron . . ."

"Do not speak. Now I see clearly. She tries from the beginning to make me against you, while at the same time to get you to bed. And to steal the cognac from my stores. All *drei* bottles is gone."

"She needs a drink. At night, Matron. To make her sleep."

"Ach, it is not that she needs for sleep! No, it is not forgivable. Especially since in her haste to snatch I think she break the vacuum *Flasche*."

Put like that, the picture looked black. Undeniably there was some justification for this point of view. One way or another, with all these complex motives, Davigan had tied herself up in a nasty tangle. I put down the tray and studied the chrysanthemums, wondering how, or if, I could unravel it.

"All was in order vith us before that voman came. I managed you well. And it will return ven she is gone, vich must be at once. Yes, she must go, and with the boy—now especially that, for your thanks, he is besser."

"But what's going to happen to her? She hasn't got a bean."

"At the beginning, to show she is good *Hausfrau*, she tells me she has the offer to keep the home of some doctor."

"Dr. Ennis?"

"That is the name."

So in every way I was off the hook. I ought to feel relieved.

"I appreciate your . . . your kindness to me, Matron," I said. "Still . . . don't you think you should be equally generous to her?"

"Vy do you ask? For veeks you try to send her home."

"I was thinking of the hospital . . . treatment, for Daniel," I said weakly.

"Then he shall be at home there to have it, at the Spital you already recommended, vich is goot. As for her, no matter, since all the blame is for her. She must go."

What could I say? I was getting exactly what I wanted. I was in the clear. At one stroke I was rid of that nasty blot on my copybook. Somehow it did not feel so good. But I was in the hole, over the barrel, there was no way out.

"You must tell her," I said finally. *That* I couldn't face.

"I go to her directly. And you vill telephone the Flughafen for places. For the same day that we are sending Higgins and the Jamieson girl. It makes one journey for all."

She stood up and came toward me with an almost maternal yet somehow patronizing smile.

"Zo now, Herr Doktor, ve shall have goot conduct. If zo, I vish to keep you. You have skill and are clever. Zo?"

God help me, she actually patted me on the back. She *was* beginning to mother me.

I had to do it. I went into my office and rang the airport, having first thoroughly shut myself in.

I wanted no part of what might take place in the chalet although, as it turned out, there was no shindy, everything passed off in a dead calm. Zurich came through at once, and presently I was on to Schwartz, the Swiss-air clerk who usually handled the Maybelle. He knew me well, and after I'd made the reservations for the 2:10 DC 6 flight on Friday, four to Heathrow and two on to Winton by the Vanguard 4:30 connection, he held on for the usual chat.

"How is your weather?"

"Bad," I said. That's the standard opening. The Swiss enjoy themselves as the world's weather pessimists, they couldn't do without the *Föhn* in summer or the *bise* in winter.

"It will be worse. More snow coming."

"You're probably right," I said.

"By the way, Doctor." His voice took on the sissy giggle of Swiss masculine confidences. "A friend of yours keeps inquiring for you with us."

"Oh?" I said warily.

"Yes, always asking when next you are coming to Zurich." He gave his neighing laugh. "I think she misses you, that very pretty Fräulein Andersen of the Aktiebolaget Svenska Örnflyg."

Lotte, asking and missing me. It brightened me somewhat, gave me a lift, put some salve upon my ego.

"Tell her I'll be down soon. Don't say actually when. Just say in the next few days."

"Ah!" He neighed again. "You wish, *natürlich*, to surprise her."

I replaced the receiver. Lotte would take my mind off things. She would do me good. Carroll, I told myself, you'll soon be yourself again. You are, and always will be, a no good heel. It suits you, and you're dead out of character when you try to tread the straight and narrow path that leads uphill all the way.

eighteen

We were in the train, passing through Kilchberg, and rapidly approaching Zurich Central. Schwartz's forecast on the weather had been amply justified. Heavy and persistent snow had blocked the valley road above Coire, making it impossible to use the station wagon. It had been a fortunate impasse. Not only had the journey been accomplished with that ease, speed and warm comfort which marks the best railway service in the world, the SBB; beyond all this, by judicious arrangement of our seats, I had escaped the embarrassing intimacies of the small closed car. Here, Davigan occupied one of the three-seaters in front with Jamieson and Higgins, while Daniel and I faced each other on single seats at the other end of the long coach. What a relief to be spared the forced formality of those last two days—the strained attempt to put a normal face on a situation that might well have gone off like a land mine. I had to hand it to Davigan. If she had feelings she had clamped down on them hard. No signs of distress, never a word or a look that might give her away. She even had a brightly polished smile for Matron when she thanked her for all her kindness and said good-bye. Yes, she was tough, for the past forty-eight hours she had saved the Maybelle from exploding in a battlefield of recriminations, accusations and abuse.

My headache had been the brain trust, who hung on to me like a leech. Without the faintest suspicion as to why they were leaving, he still seemed to have something on his mind. Even now, crouched in his seat, he kept stealing glances at me when he thought I wasn't looking at him, and when caught at this game he sat up like a startled rabbit. His conversation, too, lacked all its usual zip. During the trip he had piped out a series of platitudes, obvious cover for some inner turmoil.

"I must say I have enjoyed my visit to Switzerland, Laurence. It's such a lovely country. The snow is wonderful." And, twice repeated: "Perhaps I'll have the chance to see it again, and you, one of these days?"

It bothered me finding appropriate answers to his various speculations without stretching reality too far. But my difficulties would soon be over. You can bring yourself to a sensible state of mind if you look hard at the basic facts, among which I rated highly the acknowledged truth that you cannot relive the past. Yet what mainly buttressed me was the certainty that the late unhappy Davigan had been the victim of a wifely shove. Yes, she had certainly done him in. What could you make of such a woman? Sympathize with her? Feel sorry for her? The answer was a double negative that really hardened me. Admittedly she had her good points. She had guts and in bedworthiness she was the ultimate. But who was to know that one of these mornings you'd wake up, full of dreamy love, and find arsenic in your coffee?

We were slowing down, sliding gently into the station. I stood up and took our coats off the hooks above the seats. Davigan was helping the other two. There had been no need for me to exchange a word with her during the entire journey. I lowered the window and signaled a porter to take the suitcases, then we were out on the platform, following the trolley down Quai 7 to the Swissair terminal, which stands conveniently in the station. Another ten minutes of efficient service, we were in the airport bus, rolling along Stampfenbachstrasse toward Kloten. I had checked on flying conditions: the airport was swept clear of snow and flights were on schedule. Everything was going smoothly, everyone behaving according to the book. In less than an hour I would be rid of them. And free.

While I was on the way to congratulating myself I had, more and more, the strange and worrying suspicion that something queer seemed to be working to a head in Daniel. Still hanging on to me, though now less talkative, he was shifting restlessly on his seat, wiping the damp palms of his hands on his knees, looking up at me inquiringly from time to time. These signs of increased agitation began to worry me. Impossible for him to start another hemorrhage so soon.

He was full of my platelets. Yet if that odd chance came up, it would kill my whole program.

"Are you all right?" I asked him sharply.

"Yes, thank you. Are we nearly at the airport?"

The bus was now on the new bypass beyond Glattbrug.

"Only another ten minutes. Why?"

"I was just hoping we still had a little time together."

This silenced me. So far, although we seemed to get along on good terms, I had made no attempt to analyze his feelings toward me, beyond the fact that he apparently did not dislike me. I hoped he would not get emotional and make an exhibition of himself at this late stage. A quick glance across the aisle reassured me that Davigan at least was in full control of herself.

We made a circular sweep, drew up at the airport. While the others went ahead I waited to check the baggage. The head porter took our lot.

"Small party, this time, Herr Carroll."

"We'll have a larger one coming in before Christmas. At least thirty."

"That's good. I like always these Maybelle children."

I gave him a two-franc piece. You are not supposed to tip but they like you a lot better if you do.

I went in through the automatic glass doors. The main hall of the airport stretches a good fifty meters toward a glass frontage overlooking the runways. On the right, a row of Swissair counters, on the left a bank, shops, coffee bar and the offices of foreign airways.

Large as it is, this section is always crowded and I seemed to have lost my party. Then, as I pushed forward I half stopped and gave out a rude word. They were standing at the Swedish counter with Lotte.

"Well, here is our good friend, the doctor. How are you, dear Laurence?"

"Still living . . . I think."

She laughed, yet studying me closely.

"Always he makes a bad joke. Did he make them with you, Mrs. Davigan, when you were together at the Maybelle?"

"Not so you'd notice." She had to answer and she was bearing up, but with a struggle.

"At least I warned you against him. I hope he did not spoil your nice holiday. I know him so well, don't I, Laurence? Well, never mind. He will tell me all when you are gone."

Damn it, even in her bad English, she was hitting at me. And she was looking stunning, smart, better than ever, a regular Dior model, putting five years on Davigan's age. And knowing it. Davigan knew it too, in her baggy old suit, with that forced expression stuck on her face. And, so help me, I hadn't noticed before, she had on the snow boots. Suddenly I felt sorry for her.

"And now, would you like coffee?" Lotte had assumed full charge of the party. "No. Then if I may have your passports and boarding cards I will show you specially to the plane."

At least she was taking them off my hands.

"You see," she went on, "since I was here to welcome your arrival I think it is only polite to send you away."

They had begun to move toward passport control when I felt the tug on my arm. I bent down, he was pulling hard.

"I want you to take me to the washroom."

It shook me. At the last gasp, was he going to have another hemorrhage?

"Come quickly then."

I took him down the short flight of stairs beyond the coffee bar into the men's room.

"In there."

He still had my arm and he pulled me into one of the cabinets with him and shut the door. He was trembling all over.

"Hurry," I said. "Get your shorts down."

"I don't need to go, Laurence. But I had to tell you. I couldn't bear to leave you and perhaps never see you again and have you feel that I didn't like you enough to tell you my secret."

In sheer surprise I sat down on the pedestal. He came close to me, his quick breath on my cheek.

"This is exactly how it happened with my father. For weeks, as the big building was being finished, he became very upset. He always took some whiskey but now he drank much more, and at home he would get angry, even shouting, that by rights the building and all the new development should have belonged to him."

He took a quick sobbing breath.

"On the Saturday afternoon when he took us up to

show us, Mother didn't want to go. He'd had a lot to drink at dinnertime. But we went. At the top he began again, about how it had all been lost. Then he shouted 'I can't stand it, and I won't. I'll show them.' Mother saw what was coming and tried to hold him, but he broke away, that's how her dress was torn, and jumped. Oh, it was horrible to see him turning over in the air."

Again that sharp, pained sob. Riveted, I could scarcely breathe myself.

"Of course everyone thought he had slipped, at least at first. Canon Dingwall has always been our friend, we went to him at once, to ask if we should speak. He heard it all, and said the best thing was to be silent, not to make Father a suicide, which would be a big scandal in the church, but to give him what he called the benefit of the doubt. And for another reason too. There was no money left, absolutely nothing. But there was an insurance policy taken in his name by Grandfather Davigan for two thousand pounds, and meant for my education . . ." he faltered, "and with a suicide it would have been no good at all."

A prohibitive suicide clause in the insurance policy and Davigan, absolutely blameless, had taken all that suspicion and blame to get the money for Daniel's education. He would never need it now. How did I feel? It is worth a guess.

He was crying now as he put out his hand. I took it and held it. I think he wanted to kiss me but that I couldn't bear. I would have felt like Judas in reverse. Suddenly from the grille in the ceiling the loudspeaker of the public address system screamed at us:

"All passengers for Swissair Flight 419 to London will now leave by Gate 8."

"Hurry," I said.

He was still holding on to me as I rushed him upstairs. Lotte had left his passport at the control. I picked it up, hurried him down, and through the lower lounge. They were waiting for us at Gate 8.

"You want to miss the flight?" Lotte said.

I shook hands with Higgins and Jamieson, then I had to face up to Davigan. Now that expression had become terribly thin, I was afraid she couldn't hold it. Yet she did, the effort, though, was wearing her out, yes, it was killing her. God, she did look old, pale, drawn and sick. We shook hands, just for the look of it. She had it all ready for me.

"Thank you for all you've done for Daniel, Dr. Carroll." She fumbled in her Swissair overnight bag. "It's been quite an experience knowing you. As we'll not be meeting again I'll give you this. I've been keeping it for you for quite a long time." She handed me a brown paper-wrapped package. "That morning you left me to go to your ship, you left this in my room as well."

I accepted it, stupidly, having no idea what it might be. Then they went through the gate. I stood there watching them go.

"Wait for me," Lotte called over her shoulder.

I sat down in the lounge and looked at the parcel. What was it? A time bomb? It didn't tick. I was not ticking too well myself. Anyway, what did I care? I

opened it. Anticlimax. It was a book, the book Dingwall had pressed on me the day of Frank's ordination.
I had walked off without it early that morning when I
took off for the boat. I put it in my pocket, Lotte was
coming back through the gate.

"Now, Laurence, what have you to say for yourself?
You've been up to some tricks. I want big explanations
before we come together again."

"I've nothing to explain . . ."

"That poor woman is breaking her heart to leave
you. The moment she was in the plane the tears began.
And terrible tears . . ."

"Not for me. The little boy is ill."

"Still?"

"Yes."

"There is more. I think you sleep with her."

"I told you, that's ancient history. You think I sleep
with anybody. And what about you?"

"Could you blame me if I do? When you leave me
so long. But I do not. That is the difference between
us. Well never mind. I still like you much and now
we are together for a nice cozy time. I must be on
duty till six o'clock—a charter coming in from Helsing-
fors. But here, take the key of the flat, go there and
wait for me."

I took the key.

"Mix the cocktails for six-thirty." She gave me that
wide seductive smile.

When she had gone I had a sudden feverish longing
to go out on the open terrace to watch the plane take

217

off, to see the last of them, but I shoved it down to that strange pain under my ribs and stifled it, swung round, made for the exit, cadged a lift from one of the Swissair bus drivers, and in twenty minutes was set down at Lotte's flat.

nineteen

For five minutes I hesitated, although I cannot explain why, walking up and down outside the entrance, then I let myself in and switched on the lights. It was at least a relief to be off the cold damp street with the dirty banked snow on either side. The apartment was as neat, warm, and hygienic as ever. She had said to mix cocktails at six-thirty. I needed one now. I went to the trolley where a handful of leftover ice cubes were still stuck together in the thermos container, broke them up and put the gin and vermouth in. If I try to describe my state of mind you may not believe me, for now that my troubles were over and I free as air, I was sunk in the worst depression that had ever blighted me. The way I had built up the case against Davigan, totally misjudged her, and parked her off like a crate of damaged goods, would be hard to live down. For the first time in many a year I felt compunction, made worse by the thought that here,

219

straight away, I had come up to go to bed with that honey-eyed Swedish troll. No, no, that was pushing remorse too far. Pull yourself together, Carroll, you need relaxation, a bit of fun, a taste of good living. No point in worrying over what has now slid away into past history. You are well out of a particularly nasty situation. And what could you do? You want to charter one of Lotte's jets and overtake them in mid-air, to say, please, I'm sorry, let's kiss and be friends? Forget it.

As I sat down and sipped my drink, I felt the bulge in my side pocket. Dingwall's book: *Collected Poems of Francis Thompson*. I vaguely remembered it: a nice volume, in a green leather binding, the pages slightly fogged from age, the typical prize they dish out to seminarians. I glanced at my watch. Almost an hour to wait and, in an effort to ease my mind, I looked for the poem Machiavelli had marked for me. That is how I thought of him now, beating the suicide class, because the end justified the means. I found it with the help of the holy picture he used as a bookmark—the Simone Martini favorite of my early years, he must have chosen it specially—and the title which I had forgotten was: "The Hound of Heaven."

I took a quick look at the first few lines.

I fled Him down the nights and down the days;
I fled Him, down the arches of the years;
I fled Him, down the labyrinthine ways
Of my own mind; and in the mist of tears

I hid from Him, and under running laughter.
*   Up vistaed hopes I sped;*
*   And shot, precipitated*
*   Adown Titanic glooms of chasmed fears,*
From those strong Feet that followed, followed after.

I stopped abruptly as it all came back to me: the empty church after Frank's ordination where I sat and read the poem through. The incident had passed completely from my mind and now I took up the book and began to read again more slowly. The more I went into it, the more I tried to stop. This was not my line in literature and not, especially, at the present time. If I had been low before, now I was sinking deeper. But I had to go on, and when I had finished it I sat there, absolutely still, stricken and bound by its beauty and mystery.

Now it was clear to me, the genesis of that phobia, my intermittent torment, that mysterious unremitting pursuit from which there was no escape. In the empty church the day of the ordination, in a highly receptive state, I had run through the poem simply to kill time, barely conscious of its meaning, and without obvious effect. My mind was filled with other problems but my subconscious had seized it, buried deeply the theme of the sinner endlessly pursued through the labyrinthine ways of life by the Man. The symbol of the Hound had stuck too, to become the signal of release. Yes, I could rationalize it all. Somehow, that did not help. It did not seem fully to be the answer, since I, too, now felt myself "*defenseless utterly . . . grimed with*

*smears,/ . . . amid the dust o' the mounded years—/
My mangled youth . . . dead beneath the heap."*

I had left my drink half finished. Mixed hurriedly,
it had done nothing for me. You can never improve
a bad cocktail by adding gin. I needed another, fresh
and strong. I got up slowly, passed through the bedroom to the bathroom and emptied the glass. As I
came back, wholly absorbed, still feeling myself *"of all
man's clotted clay the dingiest clot,"* my eye caught
the fly end of a necktie showing over the edge of a
shut drawer in Lotte's neat little Swedish chest. Absently, I fancied it must be mine. One of a pair I had
bought not so long ago at Grieder's. I pulled the
drawer.

It was not my tie. Despite my aspirations toward
the higher life, I cannot afford Countess Mara ties and
both ties now visible were thus handsomely marked
with the distinctive coronet and the initials C.M. Also
in the drawer were two superfine silk shirts, with fresh
laundry bows, very chic and handmade, with the embroidered monogram C.deV. and the neat little tab
back of the collar: *Brioni. Roma.* I stood examining
these deluxe accessories like a kleptomaniac in a department store. Maybe that "de" intrigued me. Of
course I had occasionally been a trifle suspicious of
Lotte, yet at the same time always flattered myself
I was the only current bedfellow. I closed the drawer
and took a step toward the built-in wardrobe. It was
full of her lovely clothes, possibly, I now reflected,
from C.deV., and also her lovely smell. However, one
hanger at the end provided a svelte if jarring note: a

gray pinstripe suit of the finest quality. Vulgar curiosity made me hurt myself more. I looked at the tab in the inside pocket: *D. Caraceni. Via Boncampagni, 21. Roma:* the best tailor in Italy, probably in Europe. C.deV. must be a prince, or some dirty profiteer. I had always promised myself that if ever I had real money and went to Rome to call on the Pope I would have Caraceni make a suit. Now I saw the exact suit. Alas, it was not mine.

I pushed the door to and went back to the living room. Now I made myself a real, hard drink, merely breathing the vermouth across the gin, and put it straight away down the hatch. When I had mixed another of the same I took it with me and sat down. I had taken no more than a sip when I heard the turn of a key in the Yale lock. How many keys has she, I asked myself, as Lotte breezed in?

"Well, that is pretty." She stopped short, displeased. "The guest is drinking before the hostess arrives."

"You're not a hostess now. You're a V.I.P. receptionist."

"Don't be so smart or I shall be more cross with you. Then you will be less easily forgiven."

"Forgiven for what?"

"You will hear." She came forward, threw her shoulderbag and uniform kepi on the couch, and sat down showing, as usual, that beautiful extent of beautiful leg. But tonight it did not bother me. "Now give me a quick one before I bathe and change."

I poured her the slightly watery remains in the glass mixer.

"Yes." She sipped and made a face. "I must know about your woman Davigan. Although I cannot believe it, you were sleeping with her."

"Why can't you believe it?" I didn't want to know, only to irritate her.

"Because, although it is clear she is badly in love with you, she is so unattractive. Such a little bag of woman."

"She's not in love with anyone. And she's not a bag."

"You are wrong. She is gone upon you. As for looks, she is quite worn down. Don't you notice these lines under the eyes?"

"That poor woman has had a rough life." Illogically, but for some unaccountable reason, I was beginning to get angry at this denigration of Davigan. "Especially lately. Yet it may interest you to know that at your age she was a damn sight better fitted out than you are."

"Thank you for the compliment, my Scottish gentleman." Her face and neck reddened deeply. That's the worst of these total blondes, when they flush they look coarse, like the butcher's daughter with the peroxide hair. "But let us keep to the point. Did you let me down with that woman?"

"Are you jealous?" It gave me a morbid satisfaction to lead her on.

"If you wish to understand me." She compressed her lips and faced me directly. "While I would not be so common as to have jealousy, I am fond of you and would painfully resent you making love outside the privilege of my bed."

"So you value me there . . . in that sanctuary?"

"Should I not?" She was losing control now or she would not have spoken so openly. "It is something you are very good at, the best I ever knew. Then, when you are not as you are tonight, you are nice really, and amusing with all these lies I can laugh at. Now, however, I wish the truth. Why did you sleep with Mrs. Davigan?"

I looked her in the eye.

"Why did you sleep with C.deV.?"

All the color seeped out of her skin. Now she was no longer a blonde. An albino. A long pause followed. She moistened her lips.

"Who spoke of him, Schwartz?"

I shook my head.

She tried again, bitterly.

"Someone else of my good friends at the airport?" As I made no answer she went on. "He is simply a friend. A very distinguished, elderly, quite old in fact, Italian gentleman."

"Not so old he changes his shirts in your bedroom?"

"So? You are a mean, low spy."

"Yes, I'm low. And tonight I'm not pretending to be anything else."

She made an effort to be calm.

"Come, let's forget it, Laurence. You did wrong. I did wrong. So two wrongs make a right."

"Only in Sweden," I said and stood up. "I'm going now, and I'll not be back."

"Don't . . . I'll make a little supper . . . we'll be together, just as always." She put out her arm. Trying to smile, she was offering herself. "What is the matter with you? Always you tell me you have two of every-thing for me."

"Well now I've one of nothing." I knew I was cut-ting my own throat, that I would regret it, but it had to come out.

She was silent with anger and, I think, shame. As I went through the door she said:

"Don't dare ever come back."

I skipped the lift and barged down the stairs, just in time to pick up a taxi that was discharging its pas-senger—I would have liked him to be C.deV., but he was not. I flung myself into the back and said: *"Zürich Bahnhof."* I was as mad at myself as she was with me, fully conscious that I had botched everything during the day, and was now swinging wild punches from the floor, yet somehow trying to compensate, to get the whole mess out of my system, and above all, dying for another desperately needful drink.

twenty

AT THE STATION I paid off the taxi and went direct to the *Auskunft* board. I had a vague idea that a Coire train was due to leave around seven. Hurriedly, I checked the red figures of the *rapides,* only to find that this particular evening express ran only on Saturdays. But, in the black *Abfart* column of slow, secondary trains, a departure was scheduled for 7:15. A glance at the clock showed 7:13. Support of some kind was essential, and I knew what would give me the lift I needed. I had barely two minutes to sprint to the buffet, buy a bottle of vodka and beat the gate on Quai 9 before it slammed shut.

The train, strictly non deluxe, was an *omnibus,* the cheapest and slowest form of Swiss travel, with, of course, no possibility of a *Speisewagon.* It was practically empty. Who wanted to go to Coire at this season of the year and this time of night? As we crawled through the outskirts of Zurich, snow began to fall, the large drifting flakes jaundiced by the neon lights of

227

dirty, deserted streets. With a shiver, I shot down the
blinds in the bare compartment and, without hope
and strictly against regulations, turned the heating
switch a couple of notches. It did not click. This would
be a long, sad, chilly journey, yet with commendable
Carroll foresight I had the means to anesthetize myself against the sick, despondent sense of botchery,
failure and personal disgust let loose in me this afternoon. I settled in a corner of the hard wooden bench,
pulled up the collar of my overcoat, and examined the
bottle.

The label was in German.

SUPERIOR SLOVENE VODKA
SPECIALLY FOR EXPORT

This pure vodka is made by the original
Slovene recipe entirely from rye and green rye
malt and not, as with inferior brands, from
potatoes and maize

Trust the Swiss to import the best. But a couple of
peasants were passing me on the way to the forward
coach, I shoved the bottle back into my overcoat
pocket. So now, Carroll, I thought sourly, you have a
pocketful of rye, it follows naturally, after your juvenile
maunderings, and I hope it nourishes you. It was time
to try, for now I was quite alone.

As a temperate, or at least a cautious drinker, I was
more or less unaccustomed to excess. This is the alibi
I create, like Davigan's miracle wind, to exonerate myself from the subsequent events of this inconceivable
Walpurgis night. I took out my pocketful of rye. I had

no glass, it was necessary to drink from the bottle, a difficult technique, with the short squat neck and one which, badly accomplished, made me choke and cough. Nevertheless, I managed a good slug that warmed my insides, but for the moment afforded me no alleviation of my misery which, rather, was intensified by the discovery that the Slovenes had really gone to town not on purity alone, but on strength. This stuff must be two hundred over proof and would probably rot my liver.

Yet, did I not deserve to suffer? What an S.O.B. I had been, what a Gadarene swine, what a putrefying bastard. And what a B.F. I had been to top it off by reading that bloody, beautiful poem. All Dingwall's doing of course, he had probably made a novena to have the action delayed, so it would score a bull's eye on me at the psychological moment, when I was most vulnerable.

I felt like throwing a healthy curse at the old schemer, but no, that I could never do, particularly since, after a second slug, I had begun to feel more hopeful. Carroll, I told myself, do not despair, it is always darkest before the dawn.

Thus encouraged, I took a third slug, more skillfully accomplished and with more positive results—this vodka might be unhealthy, but it had an Iron Curtain kick. The old Carroll morale began to assert itself, the blood began to pulse, the spirits rose. Yes, I could bring myself, decently, to forget it, wipe out the entire complex mess, and get myself set for the future. Life was full of mistakes, everyone made them, why should

I be the exception to the rule? We were all sinners, humanity was frail. Why mourn, why shed crocodile tears? No use crying over spilled milk, the only reasonable attitude was to wipe the slate clean and start afresh.

As the train jogged through the snowy darkness, leaving the valley behind, climbing higher toward the mountains, halting at interminable wayside stations, I continued my application to the rye, achieving not personal exoneration alone, but a state of physical and mental euphoria in which all my faculties, while somewhat blurred, seemed fired up to a point of abnormal activity. In this expansive mood my present situation in the empty coach offered neither scope nor opportunity. Conversation with the conductor, who gave me a strange look and my ticket a quick punch, proved unproductive. Song, in the circumstances, would have been an infringement of good taste. Instead, with shut eyes, rolling slightly with the movement of the train, I created a series of brilliant situations justifying my position, the most diverting set in a court specially convened at my request at the Vatican wherein, with the Pontiff's blessing, I successfully brought charges of malfeasance against Dingwall, who appeared, much to the amusement of His Holiness, in a full-dress kilt. What, I asked myself, with a grin, *is* malfeasance? Anyway, I really loved that old Highlander.

Two hours later, when I tumbled out on the deserted platform of Schlewald Dorf, leaving the empty bottle on the hat rack as a testimonial to its country of origin, I was virtually airborne, yet with a calculating and elevated perception of myself, my surroundings and my condition. This last convinced me, after a careful study of the station clock which on closer examination showed nineteen minutes past eleven, that it would be unwise to present myself to the good Matron immediately. A cooling-off period was indicated and, indeed, the Arctic blast loaded with icy flakes that tore down the deserted platform caused me a preliminary shiver. In my absence a blizzard had apparently taken over. Where should I find sustenance and shelter? As I floated off through the village, a sensation to which the deep wet snow contributed, thinking in terms of coffee, I had to admit that Edelmann's was closed. Yes, confound it, everything must now be shut and, in the wise Swiss fashion, shuttered, except the Pfeffermühle. This was an establishment that, unofficially, never closed. But there I should indubitably drink more and, rather more disconcerting, be flailed with recollections of the chess match. That match, the young participant therein and his maternal relative were henceforth to be eradicated from the tablets of my memory.

I would have to chance the possibility of Hulda staying up to wait for me. Even so, everything would be arranged to her entire satisfaction. With this in mind I set off up the hill toward the main street of the town.

It was a steep hill, ankle deep in soggy slush and where the snow, earlier, had drifted, an unwary step frequently took me in up to the knees. The wind, too, was hitting me in the teeth in an effort to knock them down my throat. Altogether, to my immense surprise, when I reached an intermediate level, I found myself gasping for breath and actually hanging on to a convenient railing. That the railing belonged to the church was ridiculous enough, but not more so than the realization that this very edifice would provide me with the respite I must have before taking off again on the higher slope to the Maybelle. As usual, it was open and received me in darkness and silence when I staggered in, animated by the feeling that I was participating in the joke of the century.

Naturally I treated myself to the front pew, sat down, and shook the wet snow off myself. Not that I minded the wet, it gave me a soft, steamy feeling, as good as a sauna—that further tickled my fancy, having a steam bath in this dark, crummy church. Yet it was not all dark, for suddenly I saw a little red light flickering like an eye. They kept it at the side underneath the bas relief on the wall. No more than a rushlight in a red glass holding oil, it still diffused a glow and I knew that, as usual, He was watching me. But tonight nothing could worry me, I had the answer to that idiotic phobia, in fact I had the answers to everything, and the situation suddenly seemed to me so amusing I broke into a loud laugh and exclaimed:

"You didn't expect to see me in here, did You?"

Naturally, there was no reply, and that put my back up. So I threw my voice over and answered for Him.

"Certainly I did not expect you, Dr. Carroll." It came back perfectly with a slight echo from the hard, granite wall. "As you are now aware, I've been following you around without much success for years. But I am only too pleased to see you."

Off I went again into a fit of laughter. This was going to be good, so I slewed round, put my feet on the seat and returned the compliment.

"You don't mean that, You're just being polite. I'm afraid I'm disturbing You."

I threw the voice again.

"It's quite agreeable to be disturbed. It's a long night here, all by Myself."

I was enjoying this, I wanted it to go on, and it did.

Me: "You mean no one looks near You all night?"

The Man: "Yes, Father Zobronski looks in occasionally. He has TB, you know, and the cough keeps him awake, so he pops in to have a word with Me."

Me: "That cheers You up?"

The Man: "Naturally. But of course I'll not have him much longer, he's booked to go next year."

Me: "He's being transferred?"

The Man: "No, buried. On the ninth of October."

I had another good laugh at this, but not quite so hearty. Why the date? This thing seemed to be getting a little out of hand.

Me: "That could be a pretty good guess, since he probably has a large cavity in one lung."

The Man: "In both lungs, doctor."

Now He was going too far, I had to slow Him down.

Me: "Please don't let us have any of that knowall stuff. While I have no wish to offend, You are . . . well . . . just a bit of stucco on that wall."

The Man: "How right you are, dear Carroll, and how I wish they hadn't stuck Me up in this half-empty little chapel. Naturally I enjoy the children, and your

233

good self, on the rare occasions when you are here, but as you surmised, it is often extremely lonely and, indeed, unrewarding."

Me: "You'd have preferred one of the larger city churches?"

The Man: "Yes, a church where I would come across some of the bigger sinners, not just run-of-the-mill transgressors like you, Dr. Carroll."

Had I said that? Like the date, it had slipped out so easily, quite unpremeditated, and it jarred me. I could barely see Him but I threw a hurt look in His direction.

Me: "Forgive me, but need we be so personal? Of course, I know You've always had a down on me."

The Man: "How wrong you are, my dear Carroll. When you were young I was quite devoted to you. And I believe you had some slight regard for Me."

Me: "I suppose so." He forced it out of me.

The Man: "You weren't afraid to look Me in the eye. You didn't try to avoid Me as you do now."

I said nothing. When I started the joke I hadn't expected it to sour off into a dissection of my character. But as such it continued.

The Man: "Indeed, on several occasions I was rather proud of you. You recollect perhaps your admirable behavior when they put you in jail for helping that unfortunate girl?"

Had Carroll said that? Of course, you fool. Don't fancy you've started any of that miraculous stuff. You're lit up with rye vodka and answering yourself back. Nevertheless, it was pretty damn queer and I felt an uncomfortable pricking of my scalp as He went on:

"But when you started slacking around in your worthy profession instead of practicing it with patience and humanity, I began to lose faith in you."

Me: "You kept after me though?" I had to keep my end up.

The Man: "Yes, I seldom give up even with the most hardened cases, and of course, on account of your birth and upbringing, you are a split personality."

He caught me there—I had to admit it.

Me: "Yes."

The Man: "So there was always the chance that your better side might prevail over your worse."

Me: "My worse!" I sat up. I was beginning to get angry.

The Man: "Oh, I don't mind your lies so much, they are often quite amusing. I could even overlook your amorous exploits since, unfortunately, although you are not particularly good-looking, you have strong sex appeal which makes many women want to sleep with you and those who don't, like your good Matron, to mother you."

This was taking me down with a vengeance—when I thought of all my techniques, my efforts to create atmosphere, the records I had bought and played. He was giving me credit for nothing. I was about to bring this up when He interposed suddenly, in a cutting voice.

The Man: "The Brahms No. 4 was the most effective, was it not? Softening and soothing. Followed by the *Saber Dance*. Wild and exciting! What a clever little sinner you have become, Carroll."

He was taking my breath away. Was it possible? He . . . no, it could only be one side of my personality fighting the other. Yet I tried to defend myself against Him.

"Can't You give me credit for being in love?"

"You have not the faintest glimmering of the meaning of that word."

And He kept pouring it on.

The Man: "No, Carroll. What I cannot forgive is your almost total irresponsibility, your lack of charity and pity, your casual indifference toward those whom you have seriously injured."

The voice—whether His, or mine, I was now too troubled to discern—had lost its calm reasonableness and hardened.

"It is this, Carroll, that has brought you to the end of your tether, and unless you amend, I warn you, in all gravity, you will be irretrievably lost."

"Lost?"

Was it my faint voice, or merely an echo? The terrible conviction had grown in me that if I was, indeed, still the speaker, He was putting the words into my mouth.

"Yes, lost, Carroll. I will spare you the spiritual implications of that word. But even in its material sense you will be lost. So far, with a good spirit, your natural gaiety, and the remnants of your early training, you have, in your own phrase, got away with it. That won't continue. Unchecked, with everything permissive, you will inevitably deteriorate. You will become a selfish, indolent, useless drifter, and later, a middle-aged, run-to-seed, used-up Lothario, bored and satiated with your own vices, tortured by memories of wasted opportunities and the knowledge that you are a failure."

I wanted to answer Him. I tried. I could not. And in the silence that followed, all at once I was afraid. For some time now the Slovene potion had not been holding me up so well and, instead, its more sinister elements were taking their toll of my insides. I felt weak, sick, and helpless. And suddenly I was conscious of the terrible stillness, cut off by the snow outside, and within an isolation, chill and morbid as the tomb. We were totally alone. We? Was I out of my mind? A fresh wave of fear swept over me when the voice said:

"Are you still listening, Carroll? Have I convinced you? Or shall I go on?"

I had to end this, or it would be the end of me. I forced myself to look toward the Man, and shouted:

"For God's sake, stop, if it's really You. And if it's me, then shut me up."

Even before the echoes died, there was a sound, as of the opening of a door, followed by a sharp current of air, and all at once the rushlight went out. The darkness that followed gripped and held me, trapped beyond time and space, in a dimension wholly unearthly and untouchable. I wanted to rise and run in the frantic effort to escape. I could not. My limbs refused to move. Then in that abysmal dark, the silence was broken by slow footsteps, advancing toward me. Fro-

237

zen with terror, I was back in that nameless street. Nearer, nearer. It was the end of the chase. I tried to cry out but no sound emerged. Deathly sick, I waited for what must come.

A small circle of light shone on my face. Zobronski was bending over me with a little pencil torch.

"Dr. Carroll . . . you . . . you are ill."

"Watch out," I croaked. "I'm going to be."

Violently, I parted company with Slovenia—there was nothing else, I had not eaten since breakfast.

"I'm sorry," I managed to gasp at last. "All over your church. I'll clean it up."

"No, no. I'll do it in the morning. I'm always up long before Mass. But . . . you must come now and I'll make you some coffee.

Coffee—he couldn't miss the smell of that pure alcohol. I let him take my arm and lead me through the sacristy. I had to be led, my legs seemed not to belong to me. In slow motion we got to his room. As I had been informed, he was poor: a cheap daybed, a wooden table, two hard chairs and a crucifix.

"Would you like to lie down?"

I shook my head and sat on one of the chairs.

He was still looking at me with inquiring solicitude.

"You came to shelter."

I had to tell someone, I was still far from being myself. I gave him it all and ended with a double reiteration.

"We talked in there, one to the other, like I'm talking to you."

He simply put his hand on my shoulder and said:

"First . . . your coffee."

He went out. I still felt as if I had just been picked up from the canvas and that I was not yet out of the ring. Zobronski was somewhere next door. I heard a long bout of deep, patient coughing—that's the big single cavity, I thought: no, from that cough it must be a double. Presently he came back with a bowl of coffee. I thought: they must drink it that way in the Polish seminaries, and it will be the same ersatz coffee. But it surprised me, it was good, and I mumbled this with my thanks.

"My great luxury," he said. "A gift from the good Edelmann's."

A pause. What would happen to me next?

"You feel better?"

"Yes . . . thank you." I even said, "Father."

Another pause. He sat down on the other chair.

"My son," he said, and went on, slowly, speaking correct, scholarly English. "I am not one to decry the miraculous. But the answer to your . . . your painful experience is very simple. You have just had a dialogue with your own conscience." He paused to suppress a cough. "It is a fearful and wonderful thing, the Catholic conscience, especially when engendered in us at an early age. You can never escape it. Even the apostates cannot quite lose it, that is why an apostate is always a creature of misery. And tonight when you were . . ." he hesitated, "overstimulated, liberated from your usual controls, your conscience took over. Normally it is we who examine our conscience. Tonight it was your conscience that examined you. And judged you."

I was silent. His explanation seemed logical but he was taking all the drama away from me. No, not quite. I could not bring up the question of that fatal date, the ninth of October, but it helped me to cling to my own view.

"And now, my son," he said with meaning, "it is evident that you are troubled. Please do me the honor to tell me."

I was altogether softened up. I was no longer Carroll, I was a dishrag that had been put through the wringer and hung up, still wet, to dry. Leaning forward with my arms on the table, I told him. There was a lot of it and he heard me in complete silence.

"Now," he said, "I will give you absolution."

"You want me to kneel?"

"No, you are still not well, I will kneel beside you."

I couldn't stop him. I shut my eyes as he murmured the words. I could not laugh this one off and, if it interests you, I did not want to.

He got up, turned away from me and coughed for a couple of minutes—he had been holding it back.

"Now I am going to telephone your good Matron to bring the car."

"She's no sort of driver," I warned him. "Even if she gets down she'll never get back."

"Then I will drive you back."

He went to telephone. It took some time, perhaps the lines were down. No, now he was talking to the Matron and, although I had lost count of time, she seemed to arrive with surprising promptitude. No words passed between us until we were in the rear seat of the Opel. I wanted to drive, but knew it to be hopeless, I had a splitting headache and was still all over the place. Zobronski insisted on taking the wheel.

"Oh, how I misjudge you," Hulda was crooning down the back of my neck. "For zo long I sit up awaiting, thinking you are in some bad place in Zurich. And all the time you, zo ill, make shelter in the church, and with prayers alzo I hear." She put an arm round my shoulders. "Now all is besser between us, *mein lieber Herr Doktor*, and ven I make you soon vell, ve vork alvays *mit grosser Freundschaft.*"

Zobronski made it at last although twice he nearly had us in the ditch. Hulda insisted he take the car back to the church. Then, her arm still mothering me, she took me to my room.

"Some goote hot suppe, *lieber Herr Doktor*, and then to your warm bed . . ."

Everything had worked out well for me in the end. She had the maternal instinct, and I could use it. Happy days were here again at the Maybelle.

twenty-one

I GOT OUT OF THE WEARY TRAIN, out of the dirty compartment, still stuffed with tunnel smoke from the Central Low Level, and went down the station steps to the sound of music.

Had the town brass band turned out for the occasion? Nothing is so welcoming, or reviving, as a rollicking Sousa march. But it was Moody and Sankey that swelled toward me, the Salvation Army lassies with tambourines and a harmonium on wheels making a circle under the damp railway arches while a stray dog, its nose stretched toward heaven, set up a sostenuto accompaniment. The Hallelujahs, I recollected, started early on Saturday afternoons and worked their way down the Vennel, arriving at Market Square around the time the pubs opened. Beyond this group there was no one under the dripping arches but a solitary porter, and no sign of a cab. I eased down my bag and addressed him.

"Any chance of a taxi?"

Supporting his back against a pillar, he was busy with a fag end, pinched between forefinger and thumb, to extract the last of the nicotine. He expectorated before replying:

"They're a' at the fitba'."

"No chance by ringing up Henderson's?"

"They're shut the Setterday afternoon."

I plucked again at the chords of memory.

"What about MacLauchlans?"

"It's a funeral parlor noo."

"So, I'll have to walk."

"Ye've said it, brother."

This fraternal greeting, though owing something to percolations from Hollywood, delivered to a sudden tambourine crescendo and lingering canine howl, was at least encouraging. I thanked him politely, picked up my bag and set off. He watched my departure with ill-concealed distrust.

Out in the open it was raining, but by local standards not more than a Scots mist. I had books in the bag which, in consequence, was of no light weight, and I was tired after a long night flight.

Why, I asked myself, was it my beastly destiny to be dragging my luggage into this drab little town where already I observed signs of hideous new construction that must destroy any native character it had once possessed. The old academy with its fine twin baronial towers of Aberdeen granite had been replaced by an office complex of glass and steel in which a few overtime clerks stirred slowly, like sad sea monsters trapped in an aquarium. And the Georgianpillared Philosophical Club to which my grandfather had belonged no longer graced the dingy street. Instead, rival chainstores displayed glaring signboards that hurt the eye.

If only some kind heart had had the thought to erect one triumphal arch, festooned with streamers and artificial roses, how different would have been my re-entry to this dismal scene. But who was to know of my return? My grandparents, the Bruces, were both gone, decently interred beneath a Celtic cross in the local cemetery. True, there remained Father Francis, and the indestructible Dingwall, but when you have made up your mind to make a crashing fool of yourself, it is wise to delay all disturbing communications. Sufficient unto the day is the evil thereof, and today the evil was of my own making.

I walked a short way further up the High Street then turned sharp left into the quieter Burnside Road, which at least still seemed unchanged. The Carnegie Library remained wrapped in its mantle of Victorian repose and beside it was the same little shop where on a Saturday night, forgetting my allegiance to the royal Bruces, I bought myself a pennyworth of hot chip potatoes. Going this way I must pass the church, but at this hour it would certainly be deserted. Shifting the suitcase to my other arm I followed the curve of the road.

Wrong again, Carroll! As I came into view of St. Patrick's a long line of cars stood in front of the entrance, a large crowd swarming round them. A funeral, probably—perhaps the old Canon had finally disproved the local myth that he was eternal. No, it was a wedding, I could spot the white ribbons on the cars, some already beginning to move away. I hesitated. Turn again, Whittington Carroll? Never. Dignity and the right of way forbade it, moreover it was a good bet that I could sneak past unnoticed in the general commotion.

I hastened my steps, but the cars were beating me, taking the turn toward the restaurant we used to call the Swank. The big one, a landalette, trailing tin cans and the motto *Just Married*, pulled away as I came directly opposite the portico and there, through the gap, so help me, speeding the departing guests, was the Reverend Francis. Out of the corner of my eye I saw him as, with averted head, disguising myself with a crouching attitude, a slight limp, and the used-up air of a traveling bagman selling cheap toiletries to unsuspecting housewives, I tried to get by unobserved.

Useless. He saw me and with a bound, left the balls of his feet and flew, soared across the street.

"Laurence!" He embraced me, for a bad moment I feared he might kiss me. He had put on weight, he was plump, and rosy, with a beatific smile, garbed in an immaculate soutane of the best material on which someone had pinned a small rosebud. I used it to ease off his ecstatic greeting.

"Isn't that contrary to canon law, Father?"

He blushed. "One of the bridesmaids insisted, Laurence."

"The pretty one?"

"They were all pretty. And of course I'll take it off before we go in."

"Go in?"

"Naturally, my dear Laurence. Ever since we heard from Father Zobronski that you were coming, the Canon has been parked in the sisters' garden, a time-table on his knees, with strict instructions that you are to be brought to him."

Well, it had to come. Better now than later. I let Frank lead me down the side walk of the church toward the convent. He was already removing the rose and transferring it to his side pocket. He would put it in his toothbrush glass in his room.

As we approached the statue of the Virgin above the grotto that marked the entrance to the garden, he murmured:

"I'll leave you here, dear Laurence. But we'll be seeing lots and lots of you now, thank God." Then in a stage whisper he hissed: "He is blind in one eye and the other is failing. He has to use a high-power magnifying glass, but don't on any account mention it. It makes him very angry."

I waited till he had gone then went toward the old, the very old, nearly blind man in the wheelchair placed in the shelter of an open, cross-latticed summer house. Now I stood before him. Did he see me or merely sense that I was there?

"Your plane must have arrived on time. You caught the 12:15 Caledonian from the Central Low Level."

"Yes, Canon."

"My calculations were correct. Always a bad train that. A workman's, isn't it?"

"Yes, Canon."

"What induced you to take that bad midnight flight from Berne? On a DC 3 too?"

Have you ever noticed how old men love to work out journeys they will never take?

"I took it because it is a dirt cheap flight."

"So you are broke, Carroll."

"Stoney, Canon," and I added: "Since you wish to insult me."

Was there a flicker of a smile over that old, that very old, gaunt face? It passed.

"Well, at all events, you are back, Carroll."

"Yes, they'd had enough of me and threw me out."

"That is one of your good lies, Carroll. Your strange Polish friend wrote me that you were pressed and pressed again to stay, both by the Matron and the committee."

I said nothing.

"By the way, how is that good father with the strange name?"

"Ill," I said, and added, watching him closely, "Very. Cavities in both lungs. In fact I'm expecting bad news about him on October ninth."

No, it meant nothing to him. He merely said:

"A pity. I should have liked to meet him. Still . . . that bad night flight . . ."

He was wandering slightly and seemed to sink into himself for a moment. I tried to lighten the interview.

"Have you had anything in the way of chess lately?"

Adding more loudly to wake him up: "Chess . . . your reverence."

He came back.

"No, my young opponent has not been getting about much lately. By the way, Carroll, they have no idea whatsoever that you are coming and I did not enlighten them."

I felt good about that and was on the point of thanking him when he added:

"Not that I wished to save for you the joyful surprise of the returned prodigal. I feared, you see, that at the last minute you might not turn up."

A pause. I made no comment. He was probably right.

"Apparently it took you some time to make up your mind. Of course, I gather you yourself were ill. A slight chill?"

I nodded—his "slight" was typical and good. He obviously knew I'd had a virus pneumonia, but I went along with him.

"Due to a sauna I took in the local chapel."

"Ah!" he said, but with infinite relish. "Doubly cleansing in such an edifice. Then you had to wait for your replacement. Three months, was it not?"

"Yes," I said, reflecting that it had also given the good Zobronski lots of time to work on me, dying on his feet, too, without even a whimper.

"Well, now that you are here, Carroll, now that through the mysterious workings of the Almighty the back door is open for you—forgive me if I bore you by recalling a remark I once thought to be appropriate —now you are going to stay. For presently you will see how much, and by whom, how terribly much you are needed. And if you fail them, and me, you are a lost soul. When I am up there, and may it be soon, I will personally arrange for your non-admission." He paused, watching me out of the corner of the one good eye. "Say something, Carroll. Are you with me?"

"Yes," I said. What else could I say to this Highland Machiavelli?

"Good. Then I want you to come here quietly on Friday afternoon, just as before. However, on this occasion you will bring with you that poor troubled woman who will soon be the mother of your second child."

What a crusher! The roof of the summer house seemed to fall on my head. Yet at the back of my mind I had feared it. Carroll the potent! Carroll the propagator of the faith. I was hooked now, bait, line and sinker. He went on:

"Father Francis does all the marriages, he loves weddings, and is a great favorite of the ladies, but this one I will do. Are you with me, Carroll? Speak, or forever be silent and damned."

"Yes," I said.

"Good. I rejoice that you are, for once, in a notably affirmative mood." He held out his hand, vaguely in my direction. I took it, full of bones and blue veins.

"Now leave me. The fat Irish sister whom I detest and who hides my snuff will be coming shortly and I need my lunch. If that's what I may call the pap they give me. God bless you, my very dear Laurence. And remember Friday."

My suitcase was at the gate. I picked it up and set

off. At first my steps were slow and pensive. The recent interview had not, to say the least, exhilarated me. Yet in that affectionate penultimate phrase I found a strange comfort. A group of men passed me hurrying to the football match. Walking with my head down, the bag dragging at my ankles, the ring of their footsteps, on the hard paving ahead, came back to me. With supreme lack of logic I thought, I have become the follower, I am no longer pursued.

Now I was at the corner of Renton Road and as I turned into that familiar byway my pace insensibly increased. Obscurely, too, my heart was beating faster. In no time at all I was there, in Craig Crescent, opposite the Ennis house, which looked seedier than of old, paint flaking off the shutters, a cracked window in the surgery annex, where a few patients had collected outside. I took it all in, and using that most obnoxious Swiss word, said to myself: "Carroll, you've made the *rundfahrt*."

I drew a deep breath, crossed the road, went up the graveled weedy path, pushed open the front door and walked straight in.

The sitting room was on the left, and Dr. Ennis was lying there, stretched out on the sofa, asleep, with his mouth open, snoring gently through his nose, his midwifery bag on the floor beside him. Despite the empty glass of his usual reviver he looked all in, his face raddled, unshaven, a little gob of mucus on his bushy moustache. Not a pretty picture, but a human one. At least it was a face I knew I could live with, and

251

K

with which perhaps, on a slack afternoon, I might go fishing in the Loch.

I turned without disturbing him and went out of the room. At the end of the hall, narrowed by an enormous mahogany hat and coat stand, on which the doctor's hats, of all varieties, sprouted like cabbages, the kitchen door was open. Still holding the suitcase I advanced and stood in the doorway. Neither of them saw me.

She was seated at the low kitchen table, wearing a slate blue working wrapper, slewed a little sideways to ease the palpable, visible bulge in her middle, one elbow on the table supporting the palm that lay against her slanted cheek, while with the other hand, which held a spoon, she was feeding Daniel from a bowl of broth. He sat close, leaning against her, with a gray shawl round his shoulders. That he'd had another bleeding was evident from his general air of apathy, a lassitude which indeed seemed to encompass and bind them. It was pure Picasso, his best blue period, and it went through me like a knife.

I put down the suitcase, my heart beating heavy in my side. They looked up and saw me. Not a sound came from either but on the child's face there dawned a look of wonder and surprise, and a pale delight. And on hers, unbelieving shock, melting slowly into a slow, single, trickling tear.

I let it last for a long silent moment, a moment for which it seemed I had been waiting all my life. Just for that one silent moment, all the sickening personality that was Carroll dropped off me and I lived a million years of pure, undefiled joy. Then I was Carroll again.

"I'm back," I said. A stupid statement of the obvious, but that is what I said.

They had begun to bang on the surgery door—presumably Ennis had been out all night at a case and had skipped the forenoon surgery altogether.

"I'd like some of that broth later," I said, adding humbly, over my shoulder, as I turned into the side passage, "if there's any left." After all, I'd had nothing but a rock-hard bun at the Central buffet.

I went down the ten worn steps into the little cubicle that was the consulting room. I put on the not altogether clean white coat that hung on the back of the door, took up Ennis's stethoscope which lay on the small falldown desk, and clipped it behind my ears. Outside, they were now using their boots on the lower panels. I took six paces through the small waiting room and threw the door open.

"What the devil do you think you're doing, making all that bloody racket? I'm the new doctor here and I won't have it. Come in quietly or I'll throw your cards back at you." Dead silence.

They came in quietly.

"Now, who's first?" I said, sitting down at the desk.

An old gammer of about seventy struggled in—black mutch, tartan plaid, worn but genteel black gloves. As she settled herself, wheezing away, I looked at her in silence, waiting for what must come, knowing her for what she was, a seasoned veteran of the welfare medical service, bursting with arthritis, neu-

253

ritis and bronchitis, with bunions and a probable vari-
cose ulcer and, from the way she sat, constipation and
piles. Could I stand it—the bitter medicine as before?
Yes, with Dingwall sitting on my neck, Frank hanging
round it, and that little package in the kitchen to be
looked after, I would have to stick it out. At least, I
would have to try.